BAD BREAK

A Lucy Guardino Novella

CJ Lyons

Also By CJ Lyons:

Lucy Guardino Thrillers:
SNAKE SKIN
BLOOD STAINED
KILL ZONE
AFTER SHOCK
HARD FALL
BAD BREAK
LAST LIGHT
DEVIL SMOKE
OPEN GRAVE
GONE DARK
BITTER TRUTH

Hart and Drake Medical Suspense:
NERVES OF STEEL
SLEIGHT OF HAND
FACE TO FACE
EYE OF THE STORM

Shadow Ops Covert Thrillers:
CHASING SHADOWS
LOST IN SHADOWS
EDGE OF SHADOWS

Fatal Insomnia Medical Thrillers:
FAREWELL TO DREAMS
A RAGING DAWN

Angels of Mercy Medical Suspense:
LIFELINES
WARNING SIGNS
URGENT CARE
CRITICAL CONDITION

PRAISE FOR NEW YORK TIMES AND USA TODAY BESTSELLER CJ LYONS:

"Everything a great thriller should be—action packed, authentic, and intense." ~#1 New York Times bestselling author Lee Child

"A compelling new voice in thriller writing...I love how the characters come alive on every page." ~New York Times bestselling author Jeffery Deaver

"Top Pick! A fascinating and intense thriller." ~ 4 1/2 stars, RT Book Reviews

"An intense, emotional thriller...(that) climbs to the edge of intensity." ~National Examiner

"A perfect blend of romance and suspense. My kind of read." ~#1 New York Times Bestselling author Sandra Brown

"Highly engaging characters, heart-stopping scenes...one great rollercoaster ride that will not be stopping anytime soon." ~Bookreporter.com

"Adrenalin pumping." ~The Mystery Gazette

"Riveting." ~Publishers Weekly Beyond Her Book

Lyons "is a master within the genre." ~Pittsburgh Magazine

"Will leave you breathless and begging for more." ~Romance Novel TV

"A great fast-paced read...Not to be missed." ~4 ½ Stars, Book Addict

"Breathtakingly fast-paced." ~Publishers Weekly

This book is a work of fiction. Any references to historical events, real people, or real locales are used fictitiously. Other names, characters, places, and incidents are the product of the author's imagination, and any resemblance to actual events or locales or persons, living or dead, is entirely coincidental and not intended by the author.

Edgy Reads
Cover design: James Egan, Bookfly Designs

Library of Congress Case # 1-1667407871

BAD BREAK

A Lucy Guardino Novella

CJ Lyons

CHAPTER 1

THE BOY WAS the most beautiful thing she'd ever seen—especially since he had no idea she was watching him. Megan stood on the balcony of their hotel room, her mom still asleep behind the sliding glass doors.

High tide had receded enough that she could spot the foam-capped breakers past the dunes beyond the hotel's pool. The sunrise sky was painted in shades of citrus as if God had awoken craving a fruit salad: a wedge of lemon yellow sun surrounded by ribbons of tangerine and raspberry clouds, the sea below the shade of blueberries with lime-green waves of grass crowning the dunes.

None of it as beautiful as the boy. He was tall, obviously older than Megan's fourteen, but she couldn't resist the sight of him. He'd strode up from the dunes wearing a wetsuit with its top peeled down around his hips, leaving his chest bare, and carrying a surfboard taller than he was. When he'd entered the pool area, he'd tilted the board upright to stand beside him. Then, in one breathtaking motion, he'd vaulted into the deep end of the pool with a sideways dive into the water, carrying the long board with him. It was the single most graceful, stunning movement Megan had ever seen. As if the water had called to him and he was part of it, returning home.

When he came up for air, he rolled onto the floating surfboard and, using one hand, lazily stroked the water, gliding over the surface, eyes closed. Megan felt something stir inside her—an unfamiliar warmth, a yearning to share the freedom he possessed.

She slid the door to the room open, careful to not wake her mom, tossed on the nicest blouse she'd brought, a gauzy swing-top that barely came down to meet the waistband of her denim cut-offs. Her best friend, Natalie, had convinced her to buy it with her birthday money despite the fact Megan usually just wore a soccer shirt or one of her mom's FBI tees. Now she was glad she'd packed the blouse. The hem swished and brushed against the bare skin below her belly button, making her feel older, maybe even kind of sexy. Slipping into her well-worn Sketchers, she grabbed her room key and a twenty from Mom's wallet, scrawled a note, and went downstairs.

The hotel was a small, three-story family-run establishment. They'd had no trouble getting an ocean-view room on the top floor since it was half vacant—tourists rarely came to Harbinger Cove in large numbers until summer, the clerk had told them last night when they checked in. It was too far out of the way, especially now that Route 17 had been expanded to four lanes, making it so much easier and faster for vacationers to bypass this secluded area of South Carolina and instead drive to Hilton Head with its fancy resorts.

No fancy resorts here in Harbinger Cove, Megan thought as she crossed through the lobby empty of people except for a sleepy-looking clerk sitting behind the front desk. The décor was last century: fake wood paneling in an unnatural shade of green, orange faux-leather furniture, lamps covered in seashells too pretty to be real. The single rack of tourist information listed attractions like the outlet mall twenty miles away on the mainland, dolphin watching cruises an hour away down in Hilton Head, historical tours two hours north in Charleston, and featured sun-faded, expired coupons for the collection of shops just across the street that included several restaurants, a small grocery store, a bunch of clothing and souvenir shops, and a bakery.

She pushed through the glass doors leading from the lobby out to the circular drive at the front of the hotel. The bakery directly across the street already filled the air with the enticing aromas of yeast, cinnamon, and coffee. Who could resist?

Her plan in place, she turned the other way and walked down the side of the hotel along the path to the pool. When she arrived, the boy had set his surfboard onto the pool deck while he swam laps, the sun now high enough to send random beams through the dune grass, sparkling like sapphires against the pool's water.

"I was just going for coffee," she called to him from the fence surrounding the pool, hoping she sounded like someone sophisticated enough to drink coffee. Actually, her parents didn't like her drinking caffeine and she didn't care for the taste of coffee. But what was she going to do, ask him to join her for a cup of hot cocoa? It was already at least seventy degrees, so much nicer than chilly, gray Pittsburgh. "How do you take yours?"

He rolled onto his back, fluttered one eye open and shaded it with a hand, water dripping over his face. His hair was dark, and he wasn't that much older than her, she realized. Maybe only a year or two. Guys didn't intimidate Megan—which was maybe part of the reason why she'd never had a boyfriend. All the guys she met ended up being simply friends.

But when you're the only girl in your black belt class—except for the one gray-haired lady older than Mom—and one of three girls on the regional co-ed all star soccer team, and you hang out with your mom's coworkers from the FBI and your dad's friends who were mostly former soldiers, you learned what guys wanted in a friend, but not how to act like a girlfriend.

It had to be about more than the makeup and heels and the coy texts her friends who were girls—and who *did* have boyfriends—obsessed over.

"Don't like coffee, but could you get me a milk?" he asked with a lazy stroke of one hand that propelled him to the side of the pool. Before she could answer, he'd rolled himself out of the water and into a sitting position, then upright to his feet in a graceful move that defied gravity. Sometimes, watching her sensei perform kata, she had that same sensation. Movement flowing in sync with nature, as if the body simply went where it was destined to go.

He propped his board up against the fence where it would be out of the way of any other early-bird swimmers, studying her as he moved. As if *he* were intimidated by *her*. Megan wasn't sure what to think of that; it left her a bit flustered.

"I saw you from our balcony," she said, mainly to fill the time and space between them. "I'd love to learn how to surf. What's it like? Do you give lessons?"

His smile was genuine. He turned his head to glance behind him at the ocean. "It's like being with God." The words were low, spoken like a prayer, and she wasn't sure if they were even directed at her. Then he bounced on his heels and turned back to her. "The waves are best at high tide, not much going on the rest of the day, I'm afraid. But if you don't mind getting up early tomorrow..."

She nodded eagerly at his invitation. "I don't mind."

"Okay, then, it's a date. How about I swap

you surfing lessons for breakfast?" He patted the hips of his wetsuit. "Left my wallet in my other pants."

"Sure. That'd be great."

They walked in companionable silence, Megan taking two strides to each of his. As they passed the hotel, she darted a glance up at her room. He noticed. "Sure your folks won't mind?"

"It's just my mom. Down here, I mean. Spring break, but Dad had a work emergency. Anyway, she's asleep." She didn't add that her mom had only fallen asleep less than an hour ago.

Her mom barely ever slept, not in the two years since she'd become head of the Pittsburgh FBI Field Office's Sexual Assault Felony Enforcement Squad, and especially not in the past three months after she was wounded in the line of duty.

Even here, a thousand miles away from home and work, on a quiet beach on an out-of-the-way island in South Carolina, she still didn't sleep, had been up all night, pacing the room, double-checking the locks on the door, shutting herself in the bathroom to call Megan's dad. When Megan had asked her what was wrong, Mom said she couldn't sleep without Dad there, go back to bed. Her voice had sounded almost normal, not like she sometimes sounded when she had a panic attack. Happily for Megan, Mom hadn't had one of those in awhile, but Megan knew from her dad's work—he was a psychologist who worked with veterans with PTSD—that the attacks could come at any time, even when you were on vacation.

The thought made Megan shake her head. Her mom, the great FBI hero, always in the newspapers or out saving innocent victims from really nasty bad guys, yet her job had left her crippled in so many ways. Not just the limp she still had from her leg injury when she'd almost died three months ago. Not just the bad dreams and night terrors and panic attacks. Everyday stuff. Like trying to smother Megan—who'd proven time and again that she could take care of herself—or always trying to protect her and Dad from what really went on at work, as if they'd never heard of YouTube or Twitter.

Sometimes, it felt like Mom didn't want Megan and Dad in that part of her life. Like she had to work extra hard, be two different people, juggling two worlds: work and home. Except those worlds kept colliding. To the point where both Megan and her dad had been placed in danger, despite Mom's best efforts.

She heard her parents talking, knew Mom was thinking of leaving the FBI. Part of Megan felt guilty—Mom was really, really good at her job, and she loved it; Megan hated to think she was leaving it because of her.

Yet most of her was angry Mom hadn't left a long time ago. Megan never, ever wanted to be someone who got so focused on her job that she didn't see what it was doing to her family. She knew that was the real reason behind Dad's "work emergency." He wanted Mom and Megan to reconnect, mend fences, heal the breach between them.

Yeah, right. Megan loved her mom, she really did. But that didn't mean she had to like her. And she sure as hell didn't want to *be* like her.

"Still," the boy said, interrupting her thoughts, "I don't want to get you in trouble or anything."

Megan smiled. Mom would have a conniption—that's what Grams used to call it—if she woke to find her gone, much less with a boy older than her. Stranger danger, red alert, just say no, all that crap.

Made being with him all the more exciting and appealing. "Don't worry. I can take care of myself. By the way, I'm Megan Callahan."

"Nice to meet you, Megan Callahan. I'm Mateo Romero." He stopped and turned, thrusting a hand out to her. She shook it, noticing the rough callouses and scratches that lined his arms. Various states of healing. Not defensive wounds. Irregular, not from fingernails or even animal claws.

They passed the beachfront mansion beside the hotel, its high wall covered with climbing roses and a flowered vine that looked and smelled a bit like honeysuckle. Mateo slowed, plucked a dead leaf from the vines, settling them back into place with a sense of ownership. If he belonged to the mansion, which had its own pool and path to the ocean, why was he rinsing off in the hotel pool?

She glanced at his wetsuit. Seams frayed, shoulders stretched out. Nope, the mansion didn't belong to him. "How old are you, Mateo?" she asked.

"Sixteen. Why?" His smile crinkled his eyes. "Too young or too old?"

"Just right for me. But kinda young to be a gardener, isn't it?"

They came to the front of the hotel and the street with the small collection of shops and eateries. It was pretty much the only shopping on the island. She and her mother had crossed four bridges—the last one a drawbridge—to reach Harbinger Cove, and even last night in the dark, Megan could tell it wasn't exactly a tourist hotspot. When she'd pulled up a map on her phone, she saw that the narrow barrier island was surrounded on three sides by wide stretches of tidal marshes and cut off from its closest neighbor by the Intracoastal Waterway. There were no more than a few dozen streets, all jutting off the one main road that dead-ended at the marina on the other side of the shopping center.

He laughed. "How'd you know? I work for my uncle's landscaping company after school and on the weekend. We do the hotel and a few other houses on this block. That's why they let me use the pool."

"I'm a pretty good observer," she said, flushing under his attention.

"Like Sherlock Holmes." He took her hand while they crossed the street, even though it was empty this early on a Sunday morning. It was a casual thing, almost a reflex like when her dad held a door open for her mom—although Mom always said that was a smart tactical move on Dad's part because it left her exposed as an easy target for anyone waiting inside.

They arrived on the other side and he dropped Megan's hand once more. She wondered if he was used to guiding little kids across the street and hoped he didn't see her that way.

She hated to ruin things so soon, but figured if he was serious about teaching her to surf, she should be up front with him—better now than when Mom found out and hunted him down to interrogate him. "Actually, it's more like my mom is Sherlock Holmes. She's an FBI Agent. You may have heard of her—she's kinda been in the news lately. Her name's Lucy. Lucy Guardino."

CHAPTER 2

THE DOG IN Lucy's dreams was a beautiful creature and she wanted to be its friend. But dreams, like wild animals, were unpredictable and no matter how she tried, sometimes they morphed into nightmares. When that happened, the dog turned into a vicious monster tearing at her flesh—like the dog in real life had, the one that had been trained by a killer.

You're in control, Nick's voice soothed Lucy's panic as the dog clamped down on her ankle and threatened to tear her foot off. Blood spewed through the air, staining the snow around them. *It's not real,* Nick insisted, using the calming tones of a therapist—usually she hated when he used that tone with her, but not now when he was leading her out of danger.

She fought her terror, calmed her breathing, and forced herself to look at the dog. It wasn't a monster, despite the blood sliding from its fangs—her blood. It was just a dog, a victim of a sadistic killer, like Lucy had almost been. Both victims. Back then. In the January cold. But not now. Now, it was April and it was hot… no, that wasn't right. April wasn't hot, not in Pittsburgh. When they left yesterday morning, there had been ice on the roads, and yet she was sweating and smelled salt, and that roar wasn't the dog panting but the sound of waves… waves? There weren't any waves in Pittsburgh…

Lucy opened her eyes and blinked at the bright sunshine angling in through the sliding glass door. The door was open, a warm breeze stirring the gauzy curtain. She rolled over, one hand searching the empty space beside her. No Nick. Right. He was at home. Just her and Megan.

She ran her tongue over the roof of her mouth, tasting bile. Another bad night. She'd thought she'd put them behind her, but after driving twelve hours yesterday, her bad leg throbbing most of the time—wait, where was Megan? She jerked upright.

The bed beside her was empty, the bathroom door open, lights off, no movement. Lucy resisted the urge to reach for her Glock on her bedside table and fought to keep her voice light as she called, "Megan?"

She clawed her way free of sweat-soaked sheets and stood up. Pain spiraled through her bad ankle as she put her weight on it, but the pain was just what she needed to clear the fog of her nightmares. She hobbled around the bed to the balcony. No Megan.

A glance at the rumpled sheets and discarded PJs on Megan's bed reassured her—Megan had left on her own, which meant that unless she wanted to spend her spring break grounded inside this hotel room she would have left a...ah, there it was on the counter of the small kitchenette, beside the coffee, ugh, not real coffee, instant, they'd have to do something about that.

Apparently, Megan already had. Mom, gone for coffee, back soon, have my phone.

Okay, then. No need to panic. Megan was fine. The coffee shop was just across the street. It was one of the reasons they'd chosen Harbinger Cove with its only two hotels and slow start to the tourist season, given that it was off the beaten path compared to Hilton Head and Savannah to the south or Charleston to the north. Nick's family had been coming here for years—called the town "quaint" and loved that the beaches were quiet and relatively free of tourists since most of the ocean-side property belonged to millionaires who rarely visited their sprawling mansions.

Lucy glanced at the bathroom, desperate for a shower to wash away the night terrors. She looked back at the note. No time written on it. What if Megan called when Lucy was in the shower? It wasn't being overprotective to ask her to pick up something to go along with the coffee, right?

She grimaced at her own indecision. Give her a hostage taker or serial killer and she could make a dozen life-and-death decisions in the time it took to chamber a round in her forty caliber Glock. But deal with her daughter who'd just turned fourteen and who seesawed back and forth between acting like a child and an adult and Lucy found herself second-guessing every move she made.

It'd been the same way with her own mother when Lucy was Megan's age. Although as a child, Lucy hadn't had to deal with the stresses Megan faced—parents whose jobs meant that, despite their best efforts, they were often absent, both physically and emotionally, and a world where violence had trespassed into their own home.

She sighed and returned to her bed, sinking onto the mattress as she reached for her phone. Megan picked up on the third ring.

"Hey, it's me," Lucy said.

"Did you get my note?" The sound of china rattling and reggae music filled the background.

"Yes, wasn't sure how long you'd be."

"Mateo is getting our food now—he knows the chef, there's this Cuban pastry he says is amazing. I'll bring you back some when we're done and then he's going to give me a surfing lesson."

Lucy blinked, looked around the room. No, this was real. Her fourteen-year-old daughter out with a man—boy—stranger.

"Back up," she snapped. "Who's Mateo? Details. Name, age, address." *Juvie record, social, GPA…*

Megan was so much like her father—a born extrovert, interested in everyone she met, and she never met anyone who wasn't a best friend within five minutes. *You can't change who she is,* Nick reminded her. At least the voice in her head channeling her husband did.

"Mateo Romero. Sixteen. He's in school and he works for his uncle's landscaping firm—hard worker, today is his only day off. He does the hotel's garden and they like him enough to let him use their pool and gym. He's a surfer and he's going to teach me. Not too much today because high tide has already passed for the morning, but after breakfast, we're going to hang out on the beach and he's going to show me the basics. Then tomorrow, he'll take me out for real." The words bubbled out of Megan without giving Lucy a chance to protest.

"We've been here less than twelve hours and you've already picked up a guy?" Lucy asked. She hated her tone—it was an exact copy of the way her own mother had sounded when Lucy was a teen and pushing boundaries. Ugh. *Not* what this week was supposed to be about. This was meant to be the break she and Megan needed to get back on even footing instead of the constant bickering that had become habit.

"What's wrong with that?" Megan sniped. "Want me to get one for you, too?"

"Megan Constance Callahan, don't you take that attitude with me. You may think that turning fourteen is the equivalent of turning forty, but—"

"No..." She surprised Lucy with her contrite tone. "You're right, Mom. I'm sorry. I was just so excited and it's so beautiful here and I really like

Mateo—you will, too, I promise—and I really, really, really want to learn how to surf."

Lucy's sigh was a mix of exasperation and exhaustion. "You finish your breakfast, bring my coffee and Mateo back, and I'll meet you both on the beach in twenty minutes."

"Thanks, Mom!"

"No promises," Lucy warned, but it was too late, Megan had already hung up. Lucy stared at her phone for a long moment before phoning home. "Do you have any idea what your daughter did now?"

CHAPTER 3

MEGAN HAD BEEN dreading Lucy's interrogation of Mateo, but for once, her mom acted semi-normal instead of being overbearing and overprotective—she didn't even "accidentally" let Mateo see the semiautomatic she carried in her bag.

Turned out Mateo had never heard of Lucy, which helped. He was even more wonderful than Megan had dreamed he'd be, talking about how his mother left Honduras alone and pregnant with him, made her way to America so her son could be born here, became a citizen, married, and helped his aunt and uncle to also emigrate. The way his eyes gleamed when he told stories about his younger cousins—all of whom he was fiercely proud and protective of—and the sorrow when he told them about his stepfather—the only father he'd known—dying when a drunk driver hit him as he crossed the highway to help an elderly couple with a flat tire.

But what really sealed the deal was when, after spending the morning showing Megan some of the basics of handling the board in the water and walking with her on the beach, Mateo excused himself to return home.

"Sunday dinner is family time," he explained. "My uncle's landscaping business runs six days a week. My mother and aunt's condo rental business means cleaning and check ins on Saturday and Sunday, so we're all always working or in school. Except for Sunday dinner."

"And time off to teach tourists how to surf," Megan added.

To her surprise, he blushed. "Actually, I was meant to be helping my cousins with cleaning the rental units, but I hate being stuck inside, especially on a day like today when I could be spending it with such a beautiful lady."

A little sappy for Megan's taste, but her mom smiled the smile she got when she and Dad cuddled on the couch watching old black-and-white movies. They walked Mateo to his bicycle and watched him strap his long board to it with practiced movements. He nodded to the mansion beside the hotel, the one they'd walked past earlier.

"I promised Pastor Fleming I'd check in on his garden and orchids today. They're out of town and he's very particular—told my uncle I was the only one he'd trust with his plants." Mateo beamed proudly. "If you'd like, when I'm done, we can go to the surf shop, find you a board and wetsuit to rent for the week." He turned to her mom. "If that's all right with you, Mrs. Callahan."

Megan loved how he called her mom by her traditional married name, despite her telling him to call her Lucy. It was always weird when Mom used her maiden name for anything other than work, made her seem more like other moms when she used Dad's name.

"Are you sure you have the time?" Lucy asked. "We don't want to take you away from school or work."

"Our spring break starts tomorrow, so no school. And my uncle," Mateo's grin widened, "he doesn't mind as long as the work gets done." He focused on Megan. "So I'll meet you here at three?"

"I'm looking forward to it. Thanks, Mateo." He rode off, his muscles flexing effortlessly as he pumped the bicycle pedals.

Best thing of all? Mateo had so charmed her mother that Lucy totally forgot about yelling at Megan for leaving this morning, much less meeting up with an older guy. Maybe this spring break with your mom thing wasn't going to be so bad after all. It gave Megan a chance to prove to Lucy that she was old enough to make her own choices, that she didn't need watching over 24/7.

Back home, any guy she might be interested in was the friend or brother of someone she already knew—Pittsburgh was such a small town that way—or worse, the son of someone her mom worked with in law enforcement. Since part of Lucy's job was to forge connections with all the local police and sheriff departments, that was a lot of someones.

Down here, she could flirt without pressure. If she made a fool of herself, no one back home would ever know. Plus, no way could things get serious, not when she was here only for a week with her mom hovering on the sidelines.

Best of all worlds, Megan thought, satisfied she'd finally found a way to parlay her mother's overprotectiveness into a positive. Not that she would ever tell Lucy that. Just like she'd never tell her father she knew his work "emergency" was a sham to get her and her mom to spend "quality" time together instead of their usual constant fighting.

Parents. She rolled her eyes. They were so transparent.

Promptly at three, Megan waited outside the gate to the Flemings' mansion. Thankfully, Lucy was taking a nap, so hadn't noticed the extra time Megan had spent on her hair—she'd inherited Lucy's long, dark curls that went frizzy with the slightest whiff of humidity and fought every effort to bring them under control—or the fact that she'd taken time to apply a little eyeliner and lip-gloss, even though she usually didn't wear makeup, only carried it because all her friends did.

The Flemings' place was some kind of modern-style architecture, all concrete and steel with angles designed to get the maximum beach exposure. The gate at the end of the drive was constructed of interwoven steel circles, more artistic than an actual barrier to entry. Through it Megan could see the empty driveway, a well-loved garden—Mateo's handiwork—along the concrete wall at the boundary between their property and the hotel, a kidney-shaped pool, and the path leading over the dunes to the beach. Mateo's bike was parked outside the open garage door, but there was no sign of him or any cars.

He'd mentioned Pastor Fleming's collection of orchids; those must be inside the house. Seemed like a pretty fancy place for a pastor. As she waited, Megan wondered what kind of congregation he led—maybe one of those TV ministries where people were always sending money?

Finally at twenty after, she tried texting and calling Mateo's cell but no answer. Had he forgotten? Then why didn't he reply to one of her texts?

Bored, impatient, and fearful she'd been made a fool, she bounced her weight against the gate. It swung open. He'd said to meet him there—maybe he'd meant inside the property?

She stepped inside. No alarms or anything, it was just another driveway that happened to lead to a really fancy, expensive house. She tried texting him once more. Nothing.

Now she was getting angry. Just because he was older than her and worked for rich people didn't give him the right to blow her off. She marched up to the front door and knocked on it. Like the gate, it was open.

"Mateo?" she called inside the house, her

voice echoing in the emptiness.

Air-conditioned air rushed out to greet her, but no signs of anyone. No sounds, no movement. She stepped into the high-ceilinged foyer, her footsteps echoing from the slate floor.

"Mateo?" she called. No answer. She stepped farther into the foyer, glanced through the arch into the living room facing the ocean, and froze.

Megan covered her mouth with one hand as the afternoon sun filtered through windows streaked with blood. Blood covered the sofas, the overturned glass tables and knickknacks, the slate floor, even speckled the orchid blossoms.

So much blood. "Mateo!" she screamed. No answer.

Panicked, she ran from the house and back to the drive. Her breath heaving through her chest, she fumbled for her phone and called the one person who would know what to do. "Mom? I need help. Something terrible has happened."

CHAPTER 4

LUCY COULDN'T REMEMBER the last time she'd indulged in the luxury of a mid-day nap. But after spending the morning soaking up the warm sunshine—80 today, almost twice as warm as back home!—watching Megan and Mateo, and stressing her newly-rehabbed ankle with a couple of long strolls along the beach, she was exhausted.

Sleep pulled her in deep with its thick, heavy tendrils. Until the sound of her phone jerked her awake with a stunning blaze of adrenaline.

"Guardino," she answered automatically, her gaze scouring the unfamiliar room for any hidden threat.

"Mom? I need help. Something terrible has happened." Megan's voice was rushed, choked with sobs.

Lucy leapt from the bed, panic charging

through her. "Megan, where are you? Are you hurt?"

"I'm at that house next door. The one Mateo said to meet him at. I'm fine, but someone's hurt."

"Mateo?" Lucy asked, already out of bed and reaching for her bag. Wallet, keys, Glock, good to go. She was out the door, skipping the elevator to use the stairs, bum ankle be damned. Halfway down the first flight, she realized she'd forgotten shoes.

"I don't know. He's not here. No one's here. Just blood. A lot of it. Too much." Her voice broke.

"Get out of the house now," Lucy ordered. "Meet me at the hotel entrance. Go now." As she scrambled down the steps, her uneven gait creating a strange echo in the concrete enclosed area, a dozen scenarios ran through her mind. Call the locals? Not if it meant disconnecting from Megan. Assess the scene first in case someone needed immediate medical attention? Go in without backup?

She emerged on the far side of the lobby and aimed for the doors leading into the bright sunshine outside. No sign of Megan. She pushed through the doors, maternal instincts warring with her training. "Megan?" she called both into the air and the phone in her hand.

A familiar set of dark curls appeared in her peripheral vision. Lucy pulled Megan to her, tight. Even as relief swept through her, she still stayed on full alert, noting how the desk clerk stared at them from inside the lobby, pivoting her head to scan the area, assessing the elderly couple driving up to the hotel entrance in a late model Cadillac SUV.

Assured there was no immediate danger, she took a moment to stroke Megan's hair, soothing it until Megan's distress had eased.

"Tell me everything."

MEGAN TOOK A few deep breaths and held Lucy's hand as she began. "I went inside the house after Mateo wasn't answering my texts and there was blood, blood everywhere."

She hated how her voice trembled, tried her best to emulate Lucy's calm.

"Did you see or hear anyone?" Lucy asked, her posture already shifting away from caring mother to can-do cop.

Megan frowned. She hated when Lucy did that—she understood why, but sometimes she needed her mom to be a mom.

"No. But I stopped just inside the door." She whirled, pulling away from Lucy. Mateo, where was he? "I shouldn't have left. What if he's lying there, bleeding, hurt?"

"You did the right thing." Lucy glanced around the hotel entrance. Not assessing the pretty purple flowers or nicely shaped shrubs. She was in red alert mode and wanted someplace safe to park Megan. As if Megan were a child. When would her mom start treating her like an adult?

"Wait here," her mom ordered. "I'm going to call the local police. While I'm on the line, I'll do a quick sweep, make sure no one needs help."

She strode away, leaving Megan behind. Even with her limp and bare feet—leave it to her mom to run to help and forget her shoes—Lucy appeared imposing. Hard to do when you were only 5'5", but when her mom was on the job, no one messed with her.

Megan watched, shifting her weight as the desk clerk helped the arriving couple with their luggage. She debated for a moment. What if Lucy did find Mateo, hurt, and needed someone to do first aid? And who knew how long the police would take in a small town like this on a Sunday afternoon? Did a tiny island like Harbinger Cove even have its own police force? The closest real town was almost twenty miles and four bridges away, back on the mainland.

Or—the thought she was trying to deny punched through to the surface—what if whoever did this was still inside the house?

It made no sense—she hadn't been quiet when she'd entered earlier. Actually, she'd screamed like a silly girl in a horror film, the one too stupid to live. There was no way if someone was still inside that they hadn't heard her. They had plenty of time to flee the scene while she went to get Lucy.

That was the logic of the situation. But every horror story turned stupid-criminal joke she'd ever heard from her mom's cop friends crashed over her. Crooks weren't just stupid—that's why they were caught, after all—they could be maddeningly blind to the obvious and do what they damned well pleased despite any consequences.

Including not fleeing a crime scene before someone's mother walked in on them.

Megan followed Lucy, hesitating at the open gate at the end of the drive, then going through, waiting a few feet away from the front door, clutching her phone as if it were a lifeline.

CHAPTER 5

LUCY CALLED 911 and explained the situation as she entered the Fleming house. She kept her phone on speaker and slid it into her shorts' pocket to free both hands to hold her Glock.

The house was silent. She paused in the foyer, the slate floor cold against her bare feet, and surveyed the bloody scene in the living room. The room faced the ocean and had high ceilings, three walls filled with windows, slate floors, large white leather couches, a TV bigger than a school chalkboard, and a rainbow of orchids flowing from shelves, hanging from wall sconces, and draped along the few tables that were still upright. Most of the furniture had been knocked out of place or turned over along with books and knickknacks that had been scattered throughout the room.

No sign of a body. No sign that any injured

party had been stationary long enough to allow blood to puddle. Instead, blood streamed like confetti across the otherwise pristine white surfaces.

As she stood, allowing the house settle around her, random sounds cut through her adrenaline. The clack of an icemaker coming from down the hall. The whish of the overhead ceiling fans with their large, palmetto-shaped blades. The stir of air slipping cold from the vents. Nothing human.

She cleared the first floor; the blood appeared to be confined to the living area, culminating in a chef's knife lying in a pool of smeared blood as if dropped, a clear thumbprint visible on its stainless steel handle.

There was no blood in the hall or on the steps, the family photos arranged on the stairwell wall were undisturbed and revealed a couple in their late forties or early fifties, both trim and smiling. Several photos of them on a cabin cruiser, him wearing a captain's cap and looking bashful about it. Wedding photos, photos of the wife when she was young with an older girl blowing out birthday candles, shots of the husband and wife with friends and family at celebrations on the beach and around the pool in their backyard, and photos of the husband preaching and hugging grateful parishioners. Two lifetimes collected for display. With no clues as to what they might have done to invite bloodshed and violence into their home.

On the second floor, she found three bedrooms, none with any signs of disturbance, and a fourth that was a home office. Here there were more signs of a struggle but the only blood was a palm print on a piece of paper lying below an empty wall safe. On the paper was a set of scrawled numbers. The combination?

Okay, then. Quite a story to tell, it seemed. She reassured the dispatcher that there were no victims on scene, and slowly retraced her steps. In the kitchen she noted that the bloody knife was part of a set. She double-checked the pantry and utility closets, making certain no one was hiding or had collapsed inside. Still nothing.

How many cuts had the victim suffered? And all of them sustained on the move since there was no pooling? Did that mean there was only one actor, chasing the victim around? No, that made no sense; the victim would have fled out one of the many doors. At least two subjects, perhaps one dragging the victim while the other slashed. Weapon of opportunity, possibly some kind of warped spree-type of home invasion where the valuables taken were secondary to the thrill of the chaos and violence?

She reached the front door and saw Megan waiting outside. Typical. She swore that girl only heard every other word out of Lucy's mouth—and she cherry picked the words she wanted to hear, ignoring the rest. Lucy glanced back for one last look at the scene. Bloody mess. She was glad it was none of her business.

MEGAN DIDN'T HAVE to wait long. Lucy emerged, one hand holding her phone to her ear, the other gripping her pistol. She shooed Megan back down the drive, returned her pistol to her bag, and joined Megan at the gate, hanging up when a police cruiser appeared.

"Thought I told you to wait," she said to Megan as a patrol officer stared at them through his windshield, assessing the threat.

"Did you find Mateo? Is he okay?"

Her mom frowned and shook her head. "He wasn't in there."

The officer's lips moved—talking to his dispatcher, no doubt. Finally, he left the patrol car. He was black with short-cropped hair, taller than her dad, which placed him at 6'2" at least, wearing a short-sleeved uniform shirt that revealed his muscular arms, and no hat. His sunglasses were the kind the SWAT guys Lucy trained with wore, with the same special anti-glare tint. Megan knew they cost a lot; she'd been saving to buy Lucy a pair for her birthday.

He eyed them both for a long moment, his fingers caressing the woven leather of his holster. "You the woman called in a disturbance?"

"Yes. I'm Lucy Guardino, a Supervisory Special Agent with the FBI's Pittsburgh field office. There appears to be—"

"FBI. Dispatch said you're armed?"

"My off-duty weapon is in my bag." Lucy slowly lowered the bag to the ground and stepped back. "Along with my credentials."

The officer remained beside the car, one hand on the butt of his weapon. He jerked his chin at Megan. "And this is?"

Megan opened her mouth to answer but Lucy shook her head. "My daughter. She found the scene. There's a significant amount of blood and signs of a struggle, but no one is inside."

"You went through the house?"

"To make sure there was no one needing medical attention."

He made a noise that clearly did not approve. "And you," he nodded to Megan again, "you were inside as well?"

"Yes sir. I was waiting for Mateo. He works here, but he didn't show up or answer his texts and that's his bike," she pointed to the garage, "so I went up to the door and it was open. I only stepped inside a few feet, left as soon as I saw the—"

Another car pulled up behind the patrol car, this one an unmarked gray sedan with emergency lights behind the front grill. The officer raised a hand to silence Megan as a woman in her fifties wearing a pink sundress and wide-brimmed hat like the one Megan's grams used to wear on Easter approached. She conferred with the patrol officer. His shoulders slumped and his hand came off his weapon; he even turned his back on Lucy and Megan to face the older woman. Obvious who was in charge. And it wasn't Pretty Boy.

Megan caught her mom's eye and knew she was thinking the same thing. Lucy stood with her feet planted, hands palms up, posing no threat, but Megan could tell she was getting a bit irritated by how slowly the locals were moving. Not only was it hot standing out here on the asphalt driveway, her mom was bare footed and her bad ankle was probably aching. More than that, as Lucy shifted her weight and narrowed her gaze at the man and woman, Megan had the feeling the locals were treating Lucy like this on purpose, making certain she realized her FBI rank had no standing here in Harbinger Cove.

To her surprise, Lucy glanced at Megan and gave a one-shouldered shrug. As if to say, this was all part of the game, just play along.

Stupid adults with their stupid power trips. She wasn't about to play along. Not with Mateo missing. "Excuse me, but don't you want a description or photo or anything?"

"Of who, little lady?" Pretty Boy said without looking at her. Instead he glared at Lucy as if it was her job to keep Megan quiet.

"Mateo Romero. He's missing. It could be his blood in there—if it is, then he's injured." Megan emphasized the last word. "He needs your help. Now."

Pretty Boy bristled at that but the older woman simply smiled indulgently, as if Megan were a child. She turned to Lucy. "Officer Gant informs me you're an FBI agent?"

"On vacation."

The woman nodded. "I'm Chief Hayden. We're a small force, but I assure you we'll get to the bottom of this. In the meantime, I'm happy to secure your bag in the trunk of my car. And if you two can have a seat while we take a look inside?" As she spoke, Officer Gant stepped forward and scooped Lucy's bag from the ground. Megan glanced at her mom but then realized the two officers didn't want to leave an unsecured weapon at their backs while they went inside.

The chief opened the rear door of the patrol car in a clear invitation. Lucy simply smiled. Ignoring the chief, she took Megan's hand and led her away from the cars to a small tiled table on the other side of the drive beside the wall separating the mansion from the hotel. Lucy took the seat where her back was to the wall, allowing her an excellent view of both the drive and the front door of the house.

The corners of Chief Hayden's mouth rose as she raised an eyebrow at Lucy. Megan had done a science project last year analyzing political commercials and she recognized the same fake smile politicians specialized in. Lucy stretched her legs out as if she was settling in and getting comfy, waiting for happy hour.

"Mom," Megan said once the two police officers disappeared into the house, Officer Gant with his gun drawn, the chief following him. "No one seems to care about Mateo."

"It's not that," Lucy said. "It's a small town with a small force—they aren't used to this kind of crime. I'm guessing this Pastor Fleming probably carries some clout as well. They'll be calling him next, I'm sure."

"What about Mateo?" Megan insisted.

Lucy pursed her lips, considering. "Town this size, tourist season not officially begun, Hayden probably only has six or seven full-time officers. I doubt if she has a detective, definitely no forensic unit. Which means sheriff's department for investigation support and the state lab for crime scene processing."

"We don't have time for all that," Megan pleaded. She really didn't care about local politics. She only cared about Mateo. "Shouldn't they be calling for a search party, dogs, a helicopter?"

"Honey, I know you're worried. But these guys are doing all the right things—even if they're moving slower than you and I would like. Look around—no bloodstains outside the house, so he didn't leave on foot. Nothing between the front door and the drive, so if he went in a car, he wasn't bleeding so badly that he left a trail. And I didn't see any footprints in the blood inside the house."

Megan tried to put the pieces together. "You don't think that's Mateo's blood, do you?"

"No. But if Mateo came and saw it—"

"Then where is he?" Her voice tightened with fear. "What if he interrupted a killer? Maybe he's been kidnapped." She turned her face away, pretended to be admiring the delicate jasmine growing along the wall. Mateo's work. Could he be hurt? Or worse?

How the hell did her mom keep her personal feelings out of a case? Because Megan had to fight her tears and even more, the panic that threatened to swamp her at the thought of Mateo lying somewhere, injured, maybe dying, while she was stuck here, powerless to help him.

Lucy wordlessly gathered Megan into her arms. She didn't make any empty promises like telling Megan that everything would be all right—her mom never made promises she couldn't keep, which sometimes was irritating as hell. But right now what Megan needed wasn't promises, but something more. Something she trusted only her mother to give her.

"Find him," she told Lucy as she choked back tears. "Please, Mom. You've got to help Mateo."

Before Lucy could answer, a silver Jaguar pulled up behind the two police cars. A blonde got out, her dress the same color as the sky. She jogged up the drive, her heels slowing her down, a frown creasing her forehead and one hand pressed against her mouth. She pushed through the gate and spotted Lucy and Megan.

"Who are you? Why are the police here? Where's my husband?" The rushed questions came in a thick Southern accent that had Megan struggling to translate.

The woman aimed for the front door. Lucy stood and called out, "Ma'am—"

Too late, the woman was through the door. A moment later the screaming began.

CHAPTER 6

MEGAN HAD BEEN involved in crimes before—for some reason the psychopaths her mom hunted seemed to take their impending capture personally, and twice now had targeted Lucy's family. But she'd never experienced the frustration of watching and waiting like she was now. Everyone was moving so slowly! Didn't they understand Mateo's life was at risk?

Chief Hayden escorted Pastor Fleming's distraught wife from the house, one arm wrapped around the woman's shoulders, heads bowed together as the chief consoled her. Lucy got up and offered her seat at the table. The chief smiled her thanks.

"Now, Shelly, you need to let me and my people do our jobs." The chief took the seat opposite Megan who scooted back but was still in eavesdropping range. "When was the last you heard from Robert?"

Mrs. Fleming was older than she'd appeared at first glance, older than Megan's mom, even, mid to late forties. But still pretty—the kind of pretty that was more nurture and less nature. She sniffed and glanced up. "This morning we had breakfast. I've been at a prayer retreat in Columbia since Friday. Robert as well, but a parishioner called, needed his counsel, so he came home early." Her gaze focused on the empty driveway. "He should've been home hours ago." She frowned then her eyes widened. "Maybe that's not his blood? Maybe he drove whoever it was to the hospital? That would be just like Robert. You know that, Norah."

"Of course it would, Shelly. Do you know who he was coming to meet?"

"No." Her distraught turned the word into two syllables. "Find him, Norah. You have to promise me you'll find him. He's my world. My whole world." Another round of sobbing shook the wife. The chief patted her on the back, then disengaged herself, leaving Shelly at the table.

Megan glanced at Lucy, panicked at being left with the crying wife, and bolted from the table. The chief joined them, beckoning them to walk with her farther into the garden. "You said you had Mateo's photo and contact info?"

"Yes ma'am. From this morning. I can send it to you." Megan scrolled to the info on her phone and forwarded it to the chief's phone.

Chief Hayden held her hat in place with one

hand as the breeze kicked up and her phone in the other. "When I was starting out in this job, we thought being able to get a fax was cutting edge. Who knew I'd be running investigations from a phone smaller than my wallet?"

"We were with Mateo until 11:30 this morning," Lucy volunteered. "He left to go home for Sunday dinner."

Hayden glanced at Mateo's photo and nodded in recognition. "One of the Romero Landscaping boys. They do good work. Never had any run-ins with the family before." She turned to Megan. "He told you to meet him here?"

"He said he had to take care of Pastor Fleming's orchids, that they were out of town and only trusted him. I guess they're kind of fussy or something." She glanced back at the wife who was still bent over the table, shoulders shaking. "When I got here, I waited outside the gate but he never showed, so I texted a few times and tried to call, but no answer."

"So you didn't see him arrive? Or anyone leave the property?"

"No, ma'am. Just his bike parked in front of the garage." She nodded to the empty garage.

"Did you hear anything from inside the property? See anyone? Sense movement in the house?"

Megan shook her head. "Nothing. When I went to the door, it was open. I stepped inside—just a few feet, stopped once I saw..."

Hayden nodded. "Thanks, Megan. That's

been very helpful." She glanced up as Officer Gant emerged from the back door of the house, approaching them on the patio.

The afternoon light cast this part of the house in shadow, making the blood streaking the windows appear black. Megan shivered, curled her arms around her chest and turned her back to the house. There was a path leading over the dunes to the ocean, its bright blue sparked gold by the sun. Hard to believe anything bad could happen on such a beautiful day.

"Someone lost a helluva lot of blood," Gant said. "And the safe's door is open, contents missing. Chief, you think this Romero kid could've tortured Pastor Fleming for the combination?"

The chief frowned, mirroring Lucy's look of consternation at the wild theorizing without facts.

"Mateo would never—" Megan protested before Lucy nudged her into silence.

"Get a BOLO out on Mateo Romero as well as Pastor Fleming," the chief ordered. "Alert the county sheriff. We'll need to get the state crime techs out as well."

"Will do. But," Gant rocked back on his heels as if he was the one in charge, "sure seems pretty clear cut what happened here."

Lucy's lips tightened. Megan knew her mother was itching to jump in and take charge but not only did she have no jurisdiction, she was a potential witness. It was only as a courtesy that the locals allowed her to remain at the scene—that and the fact they needed Lucy present in order to speak to Megan since Megan was a minor.

Hah. Let Mom see how it felt, standing on the sidelines, she thought. But then her glance fell on Mateo's bike and she stifled her knee jerk reaction. This wasn't about Lucy and Megan; it was about finding Mateo safe and sound.

"We need to treat them both as a high-risk missing persons," Chief Hayden informed her patrol officer. "Get the info out ASAP."

Lucy relaxed a bit at that—Megan hated the way she could almost read her mom's thoughts. But the evidence didn't add up the way Officer Gant had seen it, with Mateo as a perpetrator. She hoped with all her might Mateo wasn't a victim. *All that blood...* She shuddered. One thing Gant had gotten right: it was too much blood.

CHAPTER 7

ALTHOUGH THE HARBINGER Cove PD didn't have the resources Lucy was used to, Chief Hayden and her force appeared to have things fairly well in hand. At least the chief didn't rush to pre-judgment like Officer Gant, who seemed to want credit for solving this case before they even knew what the case was.

Time to get Megan out of here and resume their vacation. She placed an arm around Megan's shoulders, steering her away from the house. "You have our numbers if you need anything else, Chief Hayden."

"I surely do." The chief hesitated, as if performing an internal calculation. Juggling the time it would take to finish processing the scene, how many officers she could pull in off duty, estimated time for the sheriff's department to arrive with additional manpower, hours of daylight remaining. "I'll need an official statement from both of you. Could you wait for me at the station?"

Lucy knew that wait would be longer than expected, but she also understood the pressures Hayden faced. Two high-risk missing persons in a remote area with no leads… "Of course, Chief. Let me get some shoes on and we'll head right over."

"Thanks for all your help, Special Agent Guardino." Hayden handed her a business card with the address of the police station and her phone number.

As they retraced their steps back to the drive, Lucy spotted something in one of the flowerbeds. She stopped to take a closer look without disturbing it. Megan bent over as well and Mrs. Fleming joined them, now holding a handkerchief so tightly in her hands Lucy was surprised she didn't rip it in two.

"What's that, Mom?"

"Don't touch it." Lucy glanced back at the chief. "You're going to want to take a look at this."

"Oh my goodness," Shelly Fleming gasped. Before Lucy could stop her, she lunged forward and grabbed the small black box that looked like a pager. It had a short length of tubing coming from the back of it. "Robert. Without his insulin, he'll die." She thrust the box at the chief who hurried forward with an evidence bag. "Those monsters. They've as good as killed him. He might even be dead already."

Her voice crescendoed into a shrill note of

despair. Then she glanced at her hands and noticed the blood streaking them and shrieked in terror, dropping the pump to the ground. It bounced, landing face up.

Lucy glanced down and noted the model number and insignia out of habit—it was the same type of pump a friend of hers, a Pittsburgh police detective, used. The screen was flashing a warning that it was out of insulin.

"Did your husband carry extra insulin with him or in his vehicle?" Lucy asked.

"No. Yes. I mean, he always has a backup insulin pen with him, but—" Shelly's voice trailed off. "You think he's alive? That they'd let him have his insulin?"

While the chief bagged the pump, Megan tried to comfort the distraught wife, wrapping her arms around Shelly. Lucy felt a surge of pride at the act of compassion—Megan really was her father's daughter, brimming over with empathy. Sometimes Lucy worried that empathy might make her vulnerable, but times like this, she truly admired Megan.

Lucy felt for Shelly Fleming, she really did. But she also knew the best way to help everyone involved was to stay focused and follow the evidence. Get too wrapped up in the maelstrom of emotions that random acts of violence brought with them and you could get swept out to sea.

"Is there someone I could call for you?" Megan asked Shelly.

"I'll see to her," Chief Hayden assured her.

"If you could just sit with her for a minute longer." Megan nodded and the chief beckoned to Lucy who followed her to the trunk of her Taurus where she handed Lucy back her bag and secured the insulin pump that was now evidence.

"What do you think?" Hayden asked in a low voice.

"You have an alert out for Fleming's vehicle—"

Hayden nodded. "Black BMW with vanity plates, it should show up pretty fast. If they haven't made it to the mainland and the highway already. Nice thing about only having one road off the island, we can control access. But that's a lot of blood. And did you see the safe?"

"There's no blood outside the house. From the photos I saw, Fleming wasn't a small man. It would have taken a lot to subdue him."

"Six-one, a good one-ninety or two hundred pounds. He was in great shape, too. Does those mini-triathlons. He would have gone down fighting."

"It would have taken a lot to restrain a man like that. Yet there's no drag marks."

Hayden considered that. "The Romero kid is strong, in good shape as well. And maybe he wasn't alone."

"Why carry Fleming? Why move the body at all—if there is a body?"

"Not a body, a hostage," Hayden suggested. "At least to start. Without his insulin, might still end up as a body." She thought for a moment, staring at Mateo's bike. "Kind of detail a panicked kid might not take into account."

Lucy frowned. It still didn't add up. "If Mateo is our actor and the goal was to get Fleming to open the safe, why tell my daughter to meet him here, limit his time?"

"Guess we won't know until we find him and ask."

"If I were you, I'd have crime scene techs carefully analyze the blood—not just what's on the knife and safe, but all of it. Do spatter analysis as well as a DNA profile."

"That's going to take time. Maybe more than Fleming has."

She was right. "You're tracking Fleming's phone?"

"I called it—it's in the house, slid under the sofa."

"How about Mateo's?"

Hayden shrugged. "No answer. As soon as I have a few more warm bodies, I'll get someone over there to ask permission from his family and get his carrier information. Right now, it's just me and Gant."

"Would it help if I did that for you?" Lucy hesitated to make the offer—she really didn't want to get more involved than she already was and lord knew she wanted Megan far away from an active investigation into a possible homicide, but this entire scene made no sense. She hated that, knew it would bother her until she figured out what really happened.

Hayden frowned. Lucy wasn't too surprised—local authorities often resented the FBI intruding upon their turf even when they invited the FBI in to help. But a case like this, two high-risk missing persons, violence involved, and one of them with a critical, time-sensitive medical condition—it would strain the resources of a large, well-funded police department, much less a small force like Harbinger Cove's.

"Thanks, but I'm sure we can handle it," Hayden said.

Lucy turned away, almost relieved Hayden hadn't taken her up on her offer. Then she glanced back to the garden where Megan had gotten Shelly situated at the table once more. She blew her breath out. She really didn't want to get tangled up in a case that was already a complicated mess, she absolutely did not want Megan more involved, and she understood Hayden's reluctance to allow an outsider to trespass on her case. But…

"Chief." She turned back to Hayden. "I know the pressure you're under. I'm sure your guys are totally up to the job. But there are two men's lives at stake. And this is what I do. High-risk missing persons."

Hayden squinted and it wasn't because of the afternoon sun. "What exactly is your assignment, Special Agent Guardino? Back in Pittsburgh?"

"It's Supervisory Special Agent and I run the Sexual Assault Felony Enforcement squad. We're a multi-agency, multi-jurisdiction task force working sexual predators, human trafficking, child abductions, serial killers, and—"

"Missing persons."

"And missing persons. Let me help. Until you can get more boots on the ground. You know the first few hours are the most critical."

Hayden nodded. She pursed her lips, turning her gaze on Lucy. "If you deal with sexual assaults, then you must be good at talking with victims and their families."

Every law enforcement officer's least favorite job. "Yes." Lucy glanced past Hayden to Megan and Shelly Fleming.

"I can handle Shelly," Hayden said to Lucy's relief. "But I'll need someone to work with Romero's family—without compromising the integrity of the investigation." Her tone was one of warning.

"I can do that."

"First I need their phone carrier info and permission to get a trace on Mateo's cell. That and an objective assessment of their reaction. Any hint Mateo might be involved—or anyone else along with him."

Basically, she was asking Lucy to spy on Mateo's family.

"Let me collect Megan and I'll head over there now." Lucy joined Megan and the pastor's wife. "Mrs. Fleming, we have to go now. So sorry about this."

"The good lord will see Robert home safe and sound, I just know it." She sighed dramatically and patted Megan's hand. "God bless you both for your help."

"Yes, ma'am," Megan said. "We'll keep you in our prayers."

Lucy glanced at her daughter—they weren't the most religious of families, but Megan seemed sincere. More of Nick's influence, no doubt.

She led Megan back down the drive and past the cars. As soon as they were clear, Megan turned to her. "Mom, there's something not right about this. We've got to find Mateo and get to the bottom of it."

It had been so very long since Megan had trusted her enough to ask for anything that Lucy couldn't say no. Besides, if she left Megan behind at the hotel, who knew what kind of trouble she'd end up in. Megan was headstrong—if she thought it might help find Mateo, Lucy wouldn't put it past her to play amateur sleuth on her own. Better to keep Megan with her.

"You can come with me to talk to Mateo's family. But that's the end of it. We're only going to facilitate things for Chief Hayden and the sheriff."

"That's okay. I just need to do something to help."

Lucy hugged her daughter close. "You are so much like your father."

Megan didn't pull away from the words. Which stung. Because Lucy knew full well that right now the biggest insult anyone could give Megan was to tell her she resembled her mother.

CHAPTER 8

THE ROMEROS LIVED in the center of the island, about a mile between the beach and the sound, in a modest development of older wood-frame homes that reminded Megan of their own Pittsburgh neighborhood. More so than the mansions that dotted the waterfront lots and which seemed to be competing against each other like actresses walking a red carpet—the stars wearing the designer gowns were less noticeable than the dress.

This morning when they'd walked the beach, Mateo had pointed out the variety of architectural influences. He'd said one of the reasons why so many people paid to have a house on Harbinger Cove was because they had less design restrictions than places like Hilton Head. "That and the fact we get so few tourists. People who want to protect their privacy appreciate that—and my uncle says they're willing to pay extra taxes to keep the island that way."

"We only knew about Harbinger Cove because my dad's family has been coming here for decades," Megan had told him. "Grandpap still complains his father missed out by not buying a lot down here back in the sixties."

He'd paused and smiled at her, squinting as the sun hit his eyes. "So which house would you have built? Pick any one you want."

He spread his arms wide, indicating the endless possibilities and they'd both laughed, continuing their walk and "shopping" trip. Eventually there was only one house Megan had wanted.

"That one." She pointed to a small cottage with peaked roofs, gingerbread, and a widow's walk. It was sea glass-green with cream-colored trim. Much smaller than the mansions on either side, it was what her mom called a "jewel box" of a house. The others were all spectacular in their own right, but this one felt like a home.

Mateo had grinned. "Good choice. That's the Smithstone house. One of the oldest on the beach. I helped them re-do their garden last year." He gestured to the bougainvillea draped moon gate leading to the path that protected the dunes. "It's my favorite as well."

Now, as her mom pulled into the gravel driveway leading to the two-story house where Mateo and his family lived, Megan smoothed her palms over her legs, trying to soothe the anxiety she felt any time she thought of Mateo... please, God, she prayed, don't let that be his blood. Let him be okay, keep him safe and sound.

Lucy parked between a pickup truck with ROMERO LANDSCAPING printed on the side and a van with a WELCOME PROPERTY MANAGEMENT logo. They walked to the front door but didn't make it there before it was opened and a cluster of concerned adults and children emerged.

"I'm Lucy Guardino and this is my daughter, Megan."

"Have you heard anything?" "Is Mateo all right?" "Megan, the girl from this morning?" "Chief Hayden called, said to expect you."

"How can we find Mateo?" Everyone else fell silent as the last was asked by a petite woman around Lucy's age. Mateo's mother, Megan knew instinctively. Only a mother would look so worried yet be able to push her feelings aside to do whatever it took to help. "Please. Tell me what happened to my son."

Lucy gave them all an edited, sanitized version, not mentioning the blood at the scene, only that it appeared Mateo had been at the Flemings' house and had vanished from there.

"What do you need from us?" his mother asked, her lip trembling. She seemed determined to help—as if she could provide the magic answer that would bring Mateo home safe and sound.

"Let's start with Mateo's phone," Lucy said. "Did he have GPS tracking or a finder app?"

A man, the uncle, Jorge, Megan assumed,

stepped forward. “Yes, everyone on my crew has it.”

“Okay, let’s go see where Mateo’s phone is.” Lucy and the man entered the house, leaving Megan behind on the porch, still surrounded by the rest of Mateo’s relatives. There were a few school-aged kids, his mother, and a woman who looked just like her only she was a little younger.

“I am Mateo’s aunt, Hildy, and this is his mother, Anna. Tell us,” the aunt ordered, shooing the children away as she settled Megan on a porch rocker. “What really happened? Everything. We need to know.”

The mother sat in the chair beside Megan. Megan glanced over, saw the way she was blinking fast, trying not to cry, and reached out and grasped Anna’s hand. “I’m so sorry. We’re going to find him. I know we will.”

Her mother would have disapproved of giving false hope, but what good was any hope if you didn’t share it when it was most needed? Anna squeezed Megan’s fingers tight. “Thank you.”

Megan took them through what little she knew, trying to downplay the gory details. “They said there was a safe that was empty, so I guess it was a robbery.”

Mateo’s aunt leaned forward. She was obviously the talker of the two sisters. “Pastor Fleming was robbed? And Mateo was there?” She exchanged a glance with Anna. “He must have been trying to save our money.”

“Your money?”

“Yes, the whole town’s. Pastor Fleming, he

ran a financial service, providing micro-loans to ministries in third world countries. We help them and they pay us back with interest. Our money was going to fund a mission in Rwanda."

"You were sending money to Rwanda and Pastor Fleming was helping?"

Both women beamed and nodded. "He's such a good man, has friends all over the world. Of course we couldn't do much, but we gave what we could—all our savings, ten thousand dollars. That was a year ago and tomorrow he was going to pay us and the others back. We made eighteen percent interest!"

"Who could have robbed Pastor Fleming?" Anna asked. "It must have been an outsider."

How would a tourist have known the money was in the safe? Megan thought. But instead she asked, "How many people were going to be paid tomorrow?"

They shrugged. "Everyone. Practically the entire island contributed."

"Pastor Fleming was going to pay you all in cash?"

"Yes. The churches are so tiny and in small countries, plus the banking laws—the government taxes and regulations are so complicated. This way we kept it simple for everyone."

Megan thought about the offering plate passed at Mass each week. Churches and cash, it did kind of make sense.

"Most of us were going to put it all right back in," Hildy continued. "Let our money keep doing the Lord's work. But Pastor Fleming said the bookkeeping was taking too much time and energy and he wanted to enjoy his retirement." She shook her head. "Poor man."

Anna squeezed Megan's hand again. "If the thieves got the money, then where are Pastor Fleming and Mateo?"

CHAPTER 9

LUCY LIKED MATEO'S Uncle Jorge. He was a man of few words, but answered her questions easily and gave her permission to track the company-owned cell phones, including Mateo's.

First, he showed her the room Mateo shared with two of his younger cousins. A set of bunk beds, a twin bed, two bookcases—one overflowing with children's picture books and toys, the other filled with a stack of used paperbacks, mainly action-adventure and sports figures' biographies—and a single dresser were crammed into the small space. The walls on Mateo's side of the room were filled with surfing posters, Ansel Adams' prints, and photos of interesting-appearing buildings and houses.

After showing her Mateo's room, Jorge led her to the rear of the house, past a carport sheltering two more landscaping trucks and a mountain of pine straw stacked in bales. They entered a toolshed that also served as an office with a laptop and phone perched on a workbench across from racks of carefully arranged gardening tools.

"Mateo must be all right." Jorge sounded like he was trying to convince himself of the fact as he leaned over the computer—there were no chairs. Lucy had the feeling the Romeros were the type of family who rarely sat while they worked.

"The police are doing everything they can to find him. Did Mateo have his own computer?"

"No. When he needed one, he used this one."

"How's he been acting lately? Anything strange?" She reached past him to pull up the computer's browsing history. Nothing exciting there.

"No. He gets good grades and is a hard worker. He's a good boy." Jorge's jaw clenched and Lucy intuited that he rarely gave anyone such praise in person. He turned away, typed for a few moments, then the screen filled with a map. "There. He's there. At the marina."

Not far from them—a mile and a half, on the Intracoastal Waterway. Across from their hotel and the shopping center at the southern tip of the island. "I'll call the police, let them know," she told Jorge.

"We're closer. I'm going over there myself." They left the office and went back through the house. Megan was talking to Mateo's mother and aunt on the porch but looked up as they passed.

"Where are you going? Did you find Mateo?" she asked.

"We found his phone. At the marina."

Jorge took his sister's hands and gripped them as if making a solemn vow. Then he broke away and headed toward his truck. Lucy followed. "Megan, wait here."

"No. I'm coming with you."

Lucy didn't have time to argue. The marina was a public spot on a Sunday afternoon, about as low risk as you could get. Still, she didn't like the idea of Megan being more involved.

Too late. They took off, following Jorge's truck as it spun out from the gravel drive and onto the street.

THE MARINA WAS on the other side of the shopping center at the far end of the island and faced the sheltered waters of the sound. The boats docked there ranged from small flat-bottomed bass boats to large sailboats and cabin cruisers. Only a handful of cars were parked in the gravel lot, most of them clustered around the rental kiosk. But one at the far end was a black BMW with plates that read: PASTOR1.

"That's Pastor Fleming's car," Jorge said.

"Do you know where his boat is docked?"

"No." He jogged over to the car.

Lucy debated following him but Megan was

already making her way to the rental kiosk where a lone attendant watched them. She rushed to join them.

"Have you seen this boy?" Megan asked, showing him the photo of Mateo on her phone.

He frowned, squishing his lips one way then the other. "Nope, can't say that I have."

Lucy took over. "Do the Flemings keep their boat here?"

"Of course. We're the only marina on the island." He jerked his chin in the other direction, toward the inlet leading to the sound. "That's him going out now."

Lucy squinted and shielded her eyes from the sun as she stared west into the sound. The water was a brilliant blue streaked with golden ripples. A mid-sized cabin cruiser was silhouetted against the blue of the water and sky. She couldn't make out who was at the wheel. "Did you see him? Pastor Fleming?"

"Nope. But it's his boat. Who else would be driving it?"

Damn. As soon as it reached the end of the no wake area and hit the open water, they'd lose him. She glanced around. "What's the fastest thing you have to rent?"

"Got a Formula 400 Super Sport. If you've got an operator's license." Which she didn't. "Or, if you want something that you don't need a boat license for, I got wave runners."

Perfect. "I'll take one." He fumbled below the counter for a clipboard and forms.

Lucy ignored him, grabbing a life vest from the rack beside the counter and throwing it over her head. She shook her head at Megan who was also reaching for a vest.

"Wait here. Call Hayden. Tell her to get the Coast Guard out—see if Fleming's boat has GPS," she added as an afterthought. Wouldn't that make everyone's life easier? She hung her messenger bag over her chest diagonally, made sure her phone and pistol were zipped safe inside where they'd stay as dry as possible.

"Mom, I want to—"

Lucy silenced Megan with a look. The attendant was frowning. "Now see here, I can't—"

Lucy did something she'd never done before. "FBI. Official business." She was so full of crap—if word ever got back to the office, she'd never live it down. "I'm going to find Mateo, get to the bottom of this," she promised Megan.

She climbed on board the closest wave runner without waiting for the attendant's permission. Megan cast off the line as Lucy started the engine. It'd been years since she'd driven one—last time she and Nick had taken a vacation just the two of them. Cancun. Four days of fun and sun.

Her ankle twinged as she leaned her weight on it, steering the wave runner away from the dock. So much had changed since that vacation. Megan waved. "Mom, be careful!"

The words were devoured by the roar of the engine as Lucy sped away.

Chapter 10

MEGAN WATCHED HER mom ride off on the wave runner and wasn't sure if she was angry with Lucy for leaving her behind or glad that there was a chance to save Mateo. Both. Plus, a bit of fear—for Lucy and Mateo. Whoever had taken Mateo and Pastor Fleming, it was obvious they were out of control and not afraid to hurt people to get what they wanted.

Mateo's uncle jogged over to the dock. He showed Megan a cell phone. "Found this near the car but no Mateo."

"We think he's out there. That's the pastor's boat." She pointed to the boat that was gaining speed. Lucy was standing on her wave runner, leaning forward as if trying to get the most speed possible from it.

Mr. Romero shielded his eyes from the sun.

"I can't see him."

"You with that crazy lady, Jorge?" the dock attendant asked. "What's going on?"

Megan tried her best to make out the figure driving the boat, but it was too far away and shielded by the tinted glass of the cabin. Then she saw a pair of binoculars hanging from a peg inside the attendant's shack. She grabbed them. "Okay if I borrow these?"

She didn't wait for his answer, figured Mr. Romero would do the explaining, and ran to the end of the dock. The boat operator had spotted Lucy and sped up, defying the no wake signs. Lucy was struggling with the wave runner as she drew closer to the boat's wake. Megan focused on the boat, trying to see the man at the wheel but the sun was starting to set, which meant she was looking directly into it.

Tall, lean, maybe dark-haired. That was about all she could tell for certain.

The two men joined her. "Y'all know she's not going to get very far," the attendant said. "That runner was just returned and I didn't have a chance to gas her up yet."

Megan shifted her focus back to Lucy who was bent over the controls of the runner but it was slowing, losing momentum as the boat wake tossed it. Then she looked back at the boat. The driver was making a sharp turn, aiming right for Lucy.

"He's going to run her down. Mom!" she shouted. Not as if Lucy could hear her.

"Oh damn. I'm not responsible for this," the

attendant said as the boat headed at Lucy.

They all leaned forward, straining to see everything. The boat sped up, its bow rising in the water as it charged over its own wake. Lucy's wave runner slowed, floundering in the choppy water. She kept working the controls, trying to maneuver out of the way.

Megan held her breath as the boat got closer and closer. "Mom!" This time it wasn't a shout but more of a gasp. The boat looked so much larger compared to Lucy on the small wave runner.

Finally, at the last moment, Lucy dove off the wave runner just as the boat sped over it, raising enough white water that Megan lost sight of both the runner and Lucy. She gripped the binoculars tight, straining to see Lucy come up out of the water.

The boat sped away but still no Lucy. Megan stifled a sob but it caught in her throat, making it hard to breathe. *C'mon, Mom,* she urged the empty water.

Behind Megan, Mr. Romero and the attendant got a flat-bottomed boat ready to take out. "She has a vest, I made sure of that," the attendant was saying. "I'm not liable for any of this."

"Shut up, Freddy," Mr. Romero said. The sound of an engine roared to life just as Megan saw what she'd been praying for. A spark of orange. Lucy bobbed up out of the water, coughing, waving a hand.

"She's okay!" Relief broke through her dam

of fear. Megan dropped the binoculars to wave with both hands. The wave runner floated on its side in the choppy wake. The boat was in the distance, skimming over the water, almost out of sight.

Sirens sounded behind them in the parking area, but Megan ignored them as she watched Mr. Romero skillfully maneuver the flat-bottomed boat out to where Lucy was treading water. He helped her in and began heading back to shore.

"Could've at least towed my runner for me. Now I'm gonna have to go after it myself."

Megan handed the binoculars back to the attendant with a glower. "That's my mom who almost got herself killed trying to save two men. I think your wave runner can wait a few minutes."

"She's really FBI?"

"She really is."

He hooked his thumbs in his waistband. "Well, okay, then. Guess the FBI can pay for this mess."

Megan restrained herself from slapping him. As the adrenaline fled her system, anxiety took its place. Lucy hadn't saved anyone's life. The bad guys got away. They'd lost Pastor Fleming and Mateo.

If they were even still alive.

MATEO WOKE TO darkness. And strange smells: gasoline and salt water and sweet, too sweet, lilacs.

The world churned around him, bouncing up and down, side to side, but he couldn't see why. Everything was black.

Nausea gripped him and he clenched his jaws to hold it back. He was lying—no, that wasn't right—he was sitting on a rough floor. Scratchy like sandpaper against his jeans. If only it would stop moving.

A violent roll tossed him onto his side. He tried to brace himself but his hands were caught behind him. Handcuffs? How the hell... Why couldn't he remember anything?

Panic dulled by a weird sense of lethargy made every thought a struggle, as if his mind were caught in the pluff mud that acted like quicksand in the island's tidal marshes. When trapped in pluff, you couldn't struggle. The only way out was to relax to try to float free or to have someone help pull you out.

Help. That's what he needed. He tried to call out, but his mouth was dry and only a cough emerged. Drugs. Someone must have drugged him. Was that why he was handcuffed? Was he under arrest?

Then why couldn't he see? He rubbed his face against the rough wall beside him. Felt cloth. That's where the sickly sweet lilac smell was coming from. Okay. Not blind. Just in the dark with a pillowcase or something over his head.

Cops didn't do that. What happened?

He tried to stretch his body out to explore his prison but couldn't. The walls weren't far enough apart for him to roll over without banging his shoulders and the length barely allowed him to curl up or sit halfway up, legs bent. He couldn't tell where the ceiling was.

Another sudden lurch, as if the entire vehicle—he was moving, moving fast and there was an engine roaring above the pounding in his head—had jumped a curb. Not a curb. Waves. Boat. Water.

That wasn't right, was it? He remembered being on his bike. Had to hurry, he was meeting a girl. Pretty girl. Young but interesting.

Fear surged through the fog and he sat up. Was she here, too? "Megan," he called, his voice muffled and barely carrying. "Anyone there?"

No answer, just the boat bouncing as it slowed. Think, he told himself. Remember. What happened?

Megan. He was going to meet Megan. But first… his mind sloughed through muck thicker than pluff… first… What had happened first?

A vicious roll, as the boat spun, sent him reeling, headfirst against the compartment wall. The pain flashed red against the black that smothered him.

Blood. That's what happened. He couldn't remember how or why or where or who but he remembered blood. Lots of blood.

Fear spiked through the drug-induced haze that held his mind captive. All that blood. Someone was dead.

He shuddered. And he might be next.

CHAPTER 11

LUCY KNEW SHE had many faults—leaping before looking being among the top ten—but an easily bruised ego wasn't usually one of them. Of course that was before she'd let their subject get away with two hostages, at least one potentially gravely injured. Not to mention needing to be hauled out of the water and ferried to shore sopping wet.

She was surprised Officer Gant didn't burst out laughing when she stepped back onto solid ground. But he was too busy grilling Megan.

"You couldn't see anything? Freddy said you had his binoculars."

Megan was shaking she was so upset. "I'm sorry. The sun was in my eyes and the windows were tinted. I couldn't see his face. Only that it was a man."

"Well, at least we can narrow things down. It

was a man, not a little green monster from Mars."

Lucy rushed forward to defend Megan. "She's a minor. You've no right to question her without me present, Gant. Give her a second. She'll tell you everything she knows."

Megan gripped Lucy's hand and took a breath. "I only saw one man. His head was obscured by the top of the cabin, so I'd guess he was close to six feet or taller. He wasn't black, but wasn't pale. Either very tan or brown-skinned." She thought for a moment. "I'm not sure if he had dark hair or if he was wearing a dark colored ball cap. I just saw a flash of black when he leaned forward."

Gant took notes, stopped when Megan went silent, and turned his glare onto Lucy. "And you? Sounds like you got fairly close to the boat."

"Too close—all I could see was the hull, I couldn't make out the man at all. Does it have GPS we can track?"

"Already checked. It's turned off." He narrowed his eyes. "Go change into dry clothes. The chief wants you both down at the station for formal interviews."

Lucy fished her car keys out of her sodden messenger bag—thankfully, she'd had all the compartments zipped shut before her unscheduled swim. The only thing that might be permanently damaged was her phone. "We'll be there."

Mateo's uncle followed them to the parking lot. "Thank you for trying."

"I only wish I'd been more help." Lucy thought for a moment. "Are you going back to the house?"

"Yes. The police want us there in case—" He faltered, obviously thinking of the worst reason on earth why the police would want a family handy.

"I'm sure Mateo's all right," Megan said, touching Jorge's arm.

His worry didn't ease. "They were talking like he might somehow be involved. When I gave them his phone, they said it was evidence."

"That doesn't necessarily mean evidence he committed any crime," Lucy hastened to reassure him. "But he worked at the Flemings' house on a regular basis. He might have seen something before today and not even know it was important."

Jorge frowned. "I guess. Maybe."

"I know you said Mateo didn't have a computer, but what about social media? Did he have any favorite sites?" Usually, kids Mateo's age, their online activity provided a more complete picture of who they were and what was really going on in their life than any interview with parents.

"He posted photos—loved taking pictures with his phone, especially of houses. Wants to be an architect some day."

Photos often had geotagging embedded in them. Which would give some idea of Mateo's movements. Not much to go on, but in a case like this, you never knew what might help. Jorge gave Lucy Mateo's access codes, so she should be able to take a look at his emails, texts, and any remotely stored images even though his phone was in evidence. After all, he'd already given her permission to go through everything on the cell. She made a note to grab her laptop from their hotel room. She had a feeling they'd be doing a lot of waiting as the night went on and she could work from the police station as well as anywhere.

"Thanks," she told Jorge. "I'll call if I find anything helpful."

She and Megan got into the car and headed past the shopping center to their hotel. "He's right," Megan said. "They think Mateo might be involved, don't they? Some kind of inside man?"

"Why do you think that?"

"Well, his mom and aunt told me there was a lot of money in Pastor Fleming's safe. I mean, a whole lot. Tens of thousands of dollars from these church loans he was going to pay back. Makes it easy to blame someone like Mateo who knew the money was there and had access. But," she twisted in her seat to face Lucy, "I know he didn't do it. He'd never have tortured Pastor Fleming to get the combination to the safe. He had the keys to the house—he could have easily have gotten the combination without resorting to violence. And why would he take both the pastor and the money? If he did do it, why not just run?"

Lucy noticed Megan didn't bring up what was really bothering her. "If he is guilty, would he be foolish enough to set up an alibi with the daughter of a FBI agent?"

"Right. We would have known if he was lying to us, trying to use us. Wouldn't we? Of course we would," she answered her own question.

"Mateo's not stupid. He wouldn't risk you getting the FBI involved."

"So you don't think Mateo is one of the bad guys." Lucy tried to keep the question out of her voice. If she hadn't met the boy and if he hadn't gotten Megan involved, it would be so much easier to stay objective and let the facts sort themselves out.

But Megan needed reassurance. Now. Despite her outward confidence and her aura of maturity, she'd be forever shaken if Mateo had betrayed her. If Megan couldn't trust her instincts about people, how would she ever be able to trust anyone?

That was the path Lucy walked, borderline paranoia. Only, thanks to Nick and Megan, she never made it very far, as much as she sometimes wanted to barricade her family and live by the policeman's credo of trust no one, assume nothing.

It was a life she would never wish on her daughter.

"No. I don't think Mateo is one of the bad guys," Megan finally said. "Do you?"

Lucy thought for a moment, weighing all the inconsistencies of the crime scene. "I think we need to see where the evidence leads. For me, right now, it's not pointing in that direction. But that doesn't mean we can interfere with Chief Hayden's investigation."

Megan seemed disappointed in Lucy's lack of commitment, but nodded. "Okay." She glanced at Lucy. "I'm glad you're here, Mom."

CHAPTER 12

AFTER SHE CHANGED clothes, swapping the sodden khakis and blouse she'd worn to meet Mateo's family for a pair of shorts and a polo top, Lucy stepped out onto the balcony for privacy and called Nick on Megan's phone—hers was totally soaked and she didn't want to risk turning it on until it had dried.

He wasn't happy with the direction their spring break had taken. "She picked this guy up? How could she have acted so rashly?"

Lucy found herself in the unusual position of playing therapist. It wasn't often that she was the calm one when it came to discussing Megan. "Seems like pretty normal teenage behavior to me. I mean, seriously, do you know any other girl her age whose parents subject their every choice to such scrutiny?"

"With our jobs, we're not exactly helicopter parents, able to be with her physically every moment."

"Exactly why we overcompensate. We're trying too hard to protect her, make sure we're involved in her life. But she's fourteen, that's the last thing she wants from us."

"So you're saying she's making bad choices on purpose? To rebel?"

"I'm saying when I was her age, my choices were a lot worse. To think of my poor mom, raising me alone—" Lucy blinked as her eyes misted. She'd lost her mother only a few months ago and grief still ambushed her at unexpected moments.

"Did you get involved with an older man accused of murder?" Nick's tone was pure protective paternalism—not a trace of the neutral clinical observer, the professional psychologist, or the Zen-harmony he usually brought to family discussions.

"She's on vacation, at the beach, not with her friends but with her mother, the FBI agent. Of course she flirts with the first cute guy she meets—it's totally safe. No friends around to judge her if he shoots her down, no risk of humiliation, and she knows I'd never let anything bad happen if her judgment is off."

"Sounds like it couldn't be more off. Violent, vicious, bloody murder."

"There's no body."

"Not yet. And he set her up to walk in on the crime scene? How could she not have sensed something was off with this guy?"

"You mean how could I have missed it? After all, I spent the morning with them. I gave her permission to see him this afternoon."

His silence was damning. Totally understandable—he wasn't here, he hadn't met Mateo, seen how protective he was of Megan while teaching her surfing, heard the caring tone of his voice when he spoke of his family.

"I'm not sure she was wrong," Lucy finally said. "I think he's innocent." There. She'd put her money where her mouth was.

This time Nick's silence was different. Less judgmental, more consideration. How many times had she trusted her gut instinct about a person and been right?

More importantly, how many times had she been wrong? Not many.

The silence lengthened but wasn't uncomfortable. "Okay," Nick finally said. "If you believe he's innocent, so do I. But what can we do about it? Not like murder in a small resort town is any business of the FBI. Last thing we want is Megan to try to play Nancy Drew because she thinks Mateo is getting railroaded by the locals. After all, she gets her patience from you." Translation: lack of patience.

"Guess I'll just have to work behind the scenes myself. Figure out a way to prove his innocence."

"Without letting Megan get involved."

"Right." That was going to be the tricky part.

"You're the one there. I trust your call," Nick said. "Want me to come down?"

"I'm not sure what you could do to help—other than provide distraction. I think sheer frustration at how slow a case like this can progress and the reality that we might never find all the answers are going to be the toughest things for her to handle." For Lucy as well, but that was part of the job.

"Let me see if I can get someone to cover for me." His tone was doubtful—if it had been that easy, he would have made the arrangements to start with.

Before he hung up, she had one more request. Something had been nagging at her ever since she'd seen the crime scene. "Can you give me Don Burroughs' home number?" Burroughs was her Pittsburgh Police Bureau friend who used a pump just like the one Pastor Fleming had lost. "I need to ask him about insulin pumps." Used to be she'd memorize all the contact numbers she needed—now they were all at her fingertips stored in her cell, except of course, when it was out of commission.

"I'll try my best to get down there," Nick assured her after giving her Burroughs' number. "In the meantime, watch out. For both of you."

"You know I will."

WHEN MATEO WOKE again, the boat had come to a stop, the lurching motion replaced by a gentle rocking. He felt sick but his mouth was so parched he couldn't even bring himself to throw up. There was the sound of a small engine then the boat's rocking grew stronger as someone climbed on board.

"How could you be so stupid?" a woman asked. Her voice was muffled by the fiberglass walls between Mateo's prison and the deck. He'd decided he was locked inside a storage compartment, either below deck or inside a cabin. "One simple little job, that's all you had. And you had to go and turn it into a kidnapping? What were you thinking?"

"I don't feel well." A man's voice. Not as loud, harder to make out. "Did you bring it?"

They moved away, only scattered words reaching Mateo. "FBI" was one of them—Megan's mom, was she looking for him? Or had she and Megan gone to the house to meet him and gotten hurt?

Who did all that blood belong to? Why would anyone want to hurt the Flemings?

"Thank God for my sister. I've convinced her—" The woman must have moved closer to the cabin because her voice was clear again.

"You mean blackmailed her."

"Her fault for letting all those medical bills pile up. She should be grateful we're cutting her in, letting her help us out of this jam you created. We have one chance to get this right and the timing has to be perfect. They can test for things like that."

"Like what?" The man sounded exhausted, his voice dragging.

"Time of death."

Chapter 13

MEGAN WAITED IMPATIENTLY for her mom to finish talking to her dad. She sat on her bed on the other side of the room, but didn't need to hear a word to know how things were going.

First, Dad was mad—with Megan and with Lucy. As her mom calmed him down, Lucy's body relaxed as well, until at the end, she was practically curled around the phone as if she wanted to reach through it to be with him. Which meant everything was all right.

Megan bounced to her feet and gestured to Lucy. She finally hung up and came back inside.

"What's the rush?" Lucy asked. "You know, as busy as they are, we'll just be sitting and waiting at the police station for the rest of the night."

"Maybe they found Mateo and were too busy to call us—or couldn't since you were on my phone." Which her mom wouldn't have had to borrow if she had a protective waterproof-shockproof case on her phone like the one Megan had gotten after dropping her phone one time too many on muddy soccer fields. She led the way to the door. "C'mon, Mom."

Lucy shoved her wallet, still wet from its dunking, laptop, her gun—no worries about it getting wet, Glocks were designed for that contingency—knife, their room key, and Megan's phone into her beach tote. She frowned at the way everything clunked when she lifted it, but it was better than her soaked messenger bag. "It's almost six. Maybe we should get something to eat first. It's going to be a long night."

"Can't we check in with the police first?" Last thing Megan could think about was food.

Lucy relented. "Okay." Then she surprised Megan by hugging her and planting a kiss on her forehead. "That's from Dad."

Megan edged away and opened the door. Lucy followed her out.

"He's mad, isn't he? About Mateo. Why? I hang out with older guys all the time—at soccer and Kempo and when we go shooting."

"Older guys that we know," Lucy said as they waited for the elevator. Megan knew her mom's ankle had to be hurting for her to take the elevator. Lucy had a cane in the car; Megan made a note to remind her mom that she was supposed to be using it. Not that Lucy would listen. And they called Megan stubborn.

They got onto the elevator. “I don’t think your dad’s as upset about you meeting Mateo as much as he is worried that Mateo might not be who you think he is.”

“I’m not one of your victims, suckered in by some psychopath. I know Mateo is innocent, even without waiting to see where the evidence leads.” She threw Lucy’s own words back at her. “This is still America, right? Innocent until proven guilty, right?”

“Megan. That’s not the issue. I want Mateo to be innocent as well. I especially want him and Pastor Fleming to be found safe and sound. But none of that matters compared to making sure you’re not hurt.”

The elevator stopped and the doors opened onto the parking level below the hotel lobby. Megan rushed out, heading toward the Subaru. “I’m not a child,” she tossed over her shoulder, knowing that Lucy, with her bad ankle, wouldn’t be able to keep up with her. “I don’t need you to protect me. I need you to do your job and help them find Mateo before it’s too late.”

When they arrived at the police station, a tiny single-story concrete building that smelled like a dentist office, Megan was surprised to see Mateo’s family clustered around the chairs in the front lobby. There was a reception desk manned by a gray-haired man in a police officer’s uniform but with no badge, and behind him were glass doors leading into the working area of the station, what her mom would call the bull pen.

"What happened?" Megan asked Hildy, who was perched on the edge of one of the plastic chairs, Jorge beside her, holding her hand.

"We don't know. They called us to come in, but told us to wait here. All but Anna. She's back there now." Hildy nodded to the door behind the reception desk.

"Do you think your mother can find out for us?" Jorge asked.

Lucy was already talking to the man at the desk. A reserve officer or civilian worker, Megan guessed. Maybe retired police or military from the way he kept his posture so straight despite his age, at least in his sixties. The man examined Lucy's credentials, eyed Megan, then picked up his phone. After a moment, Officer Gant appeared at the door.

Megan hastened to join her mother. Hildy and Jorge stood and stepped forward, but Gant waved them back. While he was focused on them, Megan slipped past the doorway on her mom's other side, figuring it'd be harder for them to kick her out once the door locked behind her.

Gant frowned at her but let her stay. "You can wait in there." He gestured to the open door of an interview room. "The chief needs your mom first."

Megan hesitated but Lucy nodded. "I'll be right back."

Megan crossed the bullpen to the room Gant had indicated. There were four desks all covered with evidence: crime scene photos, the note with the safe combination, the knife. Why weren't they at the state crime lab? Had the techs not arrived yet? Gant led Lucy to a small office on the far side of the desks.

There was one more interview room beside the one Megan stood outside of—empty and with the same reinforced steel door and window as her room. Multipurpose, interview and lock them up, made sense for a small town. The chief had the only proper office, glass walls like Lucy's office back home.

Chief Hayden was there now along with Mateo's mother, who sat in a straight-backed chair, face buried in her hands, shoulders heaving. Gant and Lucy joined them and the Chief turned her computer monitor around so they could all watch something. Whatever it was, it made Mrs. Romero even more upset.

Finally, Gant escorted Anna from the chief's office to the room beside Megan's. He stood, facing both of them, arms crossed over his chest as if he were guarding maximum-security prisoners. Megan didn't care. It was obvious Mrs. Romero needed help, so she strode out of her room past Gant, flinging him a glare that dared him to stop her. He surprised her by giving her a small nod of approval as she joined Mateo's mother in the room next door.

"What's happened?" she asked, crouching beside Anna's chair. "Is there anything I can do to help?"

"They're saying he did this. That tape—" She broke off, choking on tears. "It's fake. It has to be."

"What was on the tape?"

"It's a ransom demand. One million dollars or Pastor Fleming dies."

"And Mateo?" It was clear the Romeros didn't have that kind of money. "What will happen to him?"

She shook her head. "No. You don't understand. They didn't ask for any money for Mateo." She raised one hand to her mouth then lowered it again, wrapping it around her other hand on her lap. "On the tape. There's a few seconds where you can see a mirror. And Mateo. As if he's the one filming Pastor Fleming. They say he's the kidnapper. They want to arrest him."

CHAPTER 14

"WHAT CHOICE DO I have but to get an arrest warrant?" Hayden asked Lucy. "I have the kid's fingerprints in the victim's blood at the crime scene on the paper with the safe combo and the knife. Not to mention on the Pastor's insulin pump. And now this." She gestured to the computer screen where she'd frozen it on the frame that caught Mateo's face reflected in a mirror.

"Play it again for me," Lucy asked.

Hayden was rushing things, letting her emotions drive her rather than the facts. Lucy glanced around the office. On a credenza behind the desk were several photos: Hayden in uniform, with her officers, accepting an award, and several photos of Hayden with what Lucy supposed were prominent residents including one of Hayden and Shelly Fleming laughing out on a boat, the open water behind them. Hayden wore a wedding ring but there were no photos of a husband or family. In such a small community, where everyone knew each other, why did she find it necessary to keep her personal life so conspicuously absent from her office?

The video resumed, grabbing Lucy's attention. It centered on Fleming, duct tape over his eyes and restraining his wrists, sitting on a toilet in a tiny bathroom—probably on the cabin cruiser, Lucy thought. It looked like that kind of tight space. The Pastor's color was gray, his lips parched, speech strained. No obvious cuts or blood and his clothing didn't appear damaged, but the camera was shaky and mainly focused on his face.

"They want a million dollars. Deliver it and my insulin tomorrow or they'll let me—" His voice broke. "I'm going to die."

And that was it. Except for the final frames when the person manning the cell phone went to stop the recording and swung the phone just enough that a mirror on the back of the bathroom door came into view. Along with Mateo's face and upper body. His eyes were wide—Gant would probably assess him as "crazed," but Lucy thought the kid looked scared and confused.

"This whole scenario doesn't make sense," Lucy argued.

"Of course it doesn't. What would you expect from a teenaged perpetrator? Maybe it started out as a crime of opportunity that went wrong. Mateo knew he'd be the first person suspected—especially with your daughter coming any minute—so he made it look like the type of crime scene you'd only find on TV. Things just went too far, he lost control."

Hayden paused. "I'm grateful to you. Your suggestion that we test all the blood was very helpful. We found a second blood type in addition to Pastor Fleming's A positive."

"Where?"

"B negative. Pretty rare. Same type as Mateo, according to his mother. And we found it exactly where you'd expect it if he did attack Fleming."

"On the knife." It was common for attackers wielding knives to cut themselves as their grip on the blade slipped.

"Not something a subject faking a crime scene would be likely to know or think to do. So far, that's all they found. It's a lot of blood to process and I told them to check every area, not just take a random sampling." She grimaced. "I'm pretty much blowing my department's budget on this one case, so there'd better be some answers."

Lucy tried to imagine a scenario that would fit the evidence. "Staging that scene would have taken time. Mateo's uncle said he was supposed to be at Fleming's house at three, but that's also when he said he'd meet Megan."

"His family told us he left their house half past one. Even on his bike, he'd be at Fleming's place well before two. Gives him plenty of time to grab the money, get interrupted by Fleming, stage the crime scene, and grab Fleming." Hayden frowned. "Or maybe he needed Fleming to get the combination to the safe. Maybe Mateo was the one who called Fleming and asked him to come home early."

Lucy still wasn't buying it. "Okay, but if he's vicious enough to torture Fleming, why not just kill him once he got what he wanted? Why take him? A hostage adds a ton of complications and slows him down."

"A chance for more money? But that is a lot of risk. He could have just taken the money and run."

"My point exactly." Lucy paced to the doorway and looked across the bullpen to where Megan was comforting Mateo's mother. She wondered about Mrs. Fleming. Who was comforting her? Why wasn't she here? "How was the video sent?"

"Anonymous account. They texted Shelly with the link. Got so upset, we had to get her some valium. She's at my house resting now."

Lucy wished she'd been here to see Shelly's reaction to the ransom video. This whole thing didn't feel right. "Let's look at it another way. What story did our actors want to tell with the scene?"

Hayden pursed her lips. "That the Pastor didn't give up the money without a struggle. That he was hurt badly. That he might still be alive despite all the blood."

She paused, then jerked her chin, her body straightening. "Kid doesn't want to be labeled a killer. That's why he's willing to bargain for Robert's life—he never really wanted to hurt anyone and the ransom is his way out."

"I'm not sure. Still doesn't feel right."

"It does if it's a sixteen-year-old kid raised on *Criminal Minds* and *CSI*."

Megan joined them, pausing in the open doorway. Frowning at Lucy as if this was somehow all her fault. "Anna said there's a ransom video. Can I see it?"

Hayden shook her head as she reached for her phone. "I'm calling for a warrant. Thanks, Lucy. Couldn't have done it without you."

"Mom, what did you do?" Megan's voice was low but that didn't mask her anger.

Lucy moved out to the bullpen, Megan following. "Nothing. I was trying to explain to Hayden why the evidence didn't fit."

"If the evidence doesn't fit then why is she going after Mateo?"

"Because he's the only one the evidence points to."

"He's innocent. A victim." She stomped her foot. "You can't arrest him. It's wrong."

Lucy reached to comfort Megan, but she moved away. "Calm down, Megan."

"No. I won't calm down. Mateo didn't do anything. Someone has to fight for him, find out who did this."

"That's the job of the police. Not you."

Megan's eyes tightened. "Then you do it. What good is being a FBI Agent if you can't protect the innocent?"

Lucy wanted so badly to promise everything would be all right, that she had some magical ability to make bad evidence disappear and find the truth. But she didn't—she didn't even have any official standing in the case.

Despite that, she knew she'd have to try. She looked up, met Megan's gaze. "I can't make any promises—"

"Of course you can't," Megan snapped before Lucy could finish. "You never can. I hate you. I hate your job. They're going to hunt Mateo like a vicious criminal. What happens when they find him? He could get killed and it's all your fault!"

She whirled and ran through the door to the lobby before Lucy could stop her.

Chapter 15

LUCY RAN AFTER Megan. When she caught up with her in the lobby, Lucy pulled her past Mateo's family and outside to the parking lot where they could have some privacy. Last thing she wanted was to add to the Romeros' worries with her own family drama.

"Megan Constance Callahan," Lucy started. "You do not talk to me that way." Her voice had an unwelcome quaver in it—she hated being angry with Megan, hated even more the betrayal Megan's accusation carried.

Megan stood, flushed yet pale at the same time, like when she was a baby and had a fever. Lucy stepped forward, mouth open, ready to continue, when she realized she was looking Megan straight in the eye. When had her little girl grown as tall as she was?

She took another step, trembling. She was getting ready to do something she never did: make a promise she wasn't sure she'd be able to keep. Lucy wrapped her arms around her baby. "It'll be all right," she whispered. "I promise."

Megan's entire body shook with all the emotions she could not contain. Lucy pulled her tighter to her. She wished with all her heart she could somehow squeeze hard enough to return Megan to a time of innocence, that she could protect her daughter from ever knowing the ugly truth of the real world. But that was just as impossible as never breaking a promise, no matter how hard you tried.

"When you were little," she said, soothing Megan's hair as she cradled her head against her shoulder, "and you got angry or upset and felt out of control, you used to put yourself in time out."

Lucy could feel Megan's smile against her shoulder. "I'd go into my room and tear it apart. Dad used to call me Hurricane Megan."

They separated, faced each other. Lucy was glad to see Megan's color return to normal. "Remember that time when I told you to clean up the mess after one of your tantrums?"

"It was the middle of winter but I opened all the windows and threw everything out into the snow." She said it with a hint of stubborn pride.

"I came in and found you sitting on your naked mattress reading a comic book wearing nothing but your underwear." Lucy smiled at the memory, although at the time she'd been tempted to resort to her own mother's tactic of a wooden spoon judiciously applied to a bottom.

"Then Dad came in and said you had no right to complain because I was just like you. Always finding a way around the rules to do what you wanted."

Lucy smoothed Megan's hair back away from her face. "Yeah. Some days I think you got the worst of me and the best of him."

Megan considered that and Lucy braced herself for a rebuttal. But instead of the retort Lucy was expecting, Megan ducked her head down and shrugged. "Guess that's not so bad," she said, looking at the ground. "Better than what a lot of kids have."

She glanced up again, meeting Lucy's eyes with a challenge. "So what are we going to do to help Mateo?"

Lucy looked past Megan at the parking lot and realized what was bothering her even more than the crime scene and evidence. "Get in the car."

Megan rolled her eyes—oh, how Lucy hated it when she did that—but plopped down into the passenger seat and slammed the door.

The parking lot was silent. Lucy had worked multi-jurisdiction cases before, some of them in towns smaller and less equipped than Harbinger Cove. They were always a nightmare requiring coordination between agencies that didn't use the same radio codes, a mountain of paperwork and logistical support, and a command center where the troops could regroup and redeploy.

Yet, now, on the day of what she was certain was the biggest high-profile crime Harbinger Cover had ever seen, the only vehicles here belonged to Lucy, Mateo's family, Hayden and Gant's official vehicles, and one nondescript Buick. No representatives from the sheriff's department or state law enforcement, no crime scene techs securing and documenting evidence—in fact, the evidence had been laid out in the bull pen as if on display for Lucy's benefit.

What if… everything had been for Lucy's benefit? Every good crime scene analysis told a story… maybe there was a story behind this one.

Lucy hesitated. Surely her preposterous theory couldn't be right. She was torn between taking Megan back to the hotel—but no, that facility wasn't secure and she didn't want to leave Megan alone—and testing her hypothesis. There was one person who might confirm her crazy idea.

True to his word, Nick had texted Don Burroughs' number to Megan's phone. It was Sunday night, hopefully the Pittsburgh detective would be at home with his wife and two sons rather than working a case. Lucy moved to the back of the Subaru as if getting something from the trunk to hide her movements from anyone inside the station as she dialed.

"Burroughs."

"Don, it's Lucy Guardino. Did I catch you at a bad time?"

"Nope, just finished dinner." Lucy's stomach grumbled at his words—she wished she'd been able to convince Megan to grab some supper; she was starved. "What's up?"

"Need some expert advice about insulin pumps." She filled him in on the case and explained how Fleming's pump had been found empty. She gave him the manufacturer and model number. "Same as yours, right?"

"Yeah, so?"

"So our victim would have lost it no more than an hour or two before we found it, given our timeline. Shouldn't it have had insulin left in it? Or would it have all drained out when it was removed from Fleming?"

"Nope, if it's like mine, it automatically stops when it's disconnected."

"So it should have had half a day's worth of insulin in it, right?"

"Depending on what time of day your victim fills his reservoir. But most folks do it first thing in the morning or before bed, so yeah, it should have had plenty left." He paused. "You're not talking like you think this guy really is a victim. Do you think the pump was planted?"

"I'm thinking a lot of things about this scene don't add up—unless it was staged. Which means maybe Fleming isn't a victim but someone who wanted to disappear."

He made a grunting noise of agreement. "And make it look like someone else was doing the disappearing. If he uses a pump, good bet he has a duplicate with him now—once you get used to them, you never want to go back to multiple injections. I'd check that first, I was you. Plus, he must be a fairly brittle diabetic to need a specialized pump like mine."

That piqued her curiosity—special was good when tracking a missing person or a fugitive. Anything that made them stand out could create a trail to follow. "What's so special about it?"

"It's got the newest tech—monitors your blood sugar, calculates insulin dosing, sends all the info to your phone, your computer, even your doctor's office if you want. And it's designed for high-risk patients with a special safety feature. One that might let you track your guy if he hasn't inactivated it."

"Please tell me it has GPS tracking." Lucy was practically bouncing with enthusiasm.

"Yep. It's designed so if a patient hits the danger zone and doesn't respond to the pump's alarms, it sends your location to a special emergency operator. But even if he's turned off the alarm, I'll bet your tech guys could still access the GPS signal."

"I could kiss you! Lunch is on me when I get home."

"Give 'em hell, Lucy."

"Always do." She hung up, uncertain of the safest way to use Burroughs' information. Squinting at the police station and its curious lack of activity, she thought again about the incestuous relationship small town police could have with the people they were sworn to serve and protect. Sometimes that protection came at a cost—law and order sacrificed in the name of the "greater good" of the community.

She needed an outside agency, someone she could trust. And she needed to make sure Megan was safe.

Leave? Why not? She could park Megan in an anonymous hotel back on the mainland. There was nothing in their room that was irreplaceable or valuable, except maybe Lucy's phone left drying on the bathroom counter.

"Let's go," she said, joining Megan in the Subaru.

"We can't. We have to give our statements."

"We'll come back in the morning. When they're less busy."

Megan frowned and looked back at the station. "What was that call about? You know something. Why don't you want the police and Mateo's family to know?"

Chapter 16

As Lucy turned out of the police station, she did a quick mental inventory of what was in the Subaru's trunk—it was one of the reasons why she'd gotten the Legacy after wrecking her Forrester, the ability to keep items secured and out of sight. Most of their neighbors carried normal Pennsylvania-winter supplies: a small shovel, kitty litter, blanket, boots, warm socks.

Lucy's trunk had all that along with a lock box containing spare ammo for her service weapons, along with a pump action Remington 870, ballistic vest, night vision thermal/infrared monocular (a gift from some friends at the DEA, latest tech from the battlefield), handcuffs, zip ties, and combat medic kit. Stashed beside it was a go-bag with survival basics. Not much room left over for luggage, but since this was the first vacation she'd taken in years, that was the least of her concerns.

She came to the intersection with the main road that divided the island into ocean side and sound side. Turn left and she'd head north, winding across three other barrier islands and four bridges until reaching the mainland over twenty miles away. Turn right and ten minutes later, they'd be at the far end of the island where their hotel stood.

She hit the blinker to turn left.

"Mom, what are you doing?" Megan protested. Nothing got past her—often to Lucy's regret.

"I need to get you off this island. I can come back for our things later."

"That's crazy. We can't leave. Not now."

"It's not your decision." There was no traffic on the road. Lucy turned left.

Megan twisted in her seat to face her. "Pull over."

"We can discuss this later." Lucy was distracted watching all her mirrors and running tactical scenarios through her mind—hard to do when you didn't know the lay of the land as well as your opponent.

And when you weren't certain who your opponent actually was.

"No." Megan's tone was sharp. "All my life you've trained me and dad to do what you tell us to do if it's a dangerous situation. I understand that. But there's no danger now. No need to panic."

"I'm not panicking. And this isn't PTSD," Lucy added, before Megan could humiliate her by asking. "You need to trust me."

"You mean trust your gut."

"Well, yes."

Megan twisted, checking the rear window. No headlights anywhere in sight as the road curved between Spanish moss laden trees. The occasional driveway or residential lane interrupted the tree line but no human activity. "Pull in there," she indicated a narrow street that had only a few large houses, none of them with lights on. "We'll be hidden from view and you can explain what's going on."

"I'll explain once I have you safe on the mainland."

"No, Mom. Do it now. If you're going to ask me to abandon Mateo and his family, if you truly want me to be the kind of person who would betray a friend like that, then I need to understand why."

Lucy sucked in her breath, slowed the car and backed them into the street, turning the headlights off. She hated it when Megan out-reasoned her. One of the many pitfalls of having a child smarter than she was—smarter than Nick as well, which was saying a lot.

"Dad calls it tactical awareness," Megan continued. "Like when a soldier feels there's something wrong so he steps left instead of right and misses an IED. He says it's the sum of sensory perceptions and pattern recognition combining to create a quick-action reflex, instead of processing every decision step by step. But I need to understand, so take me through it the slow way, okay?"

Lucy took a deep breath and held it, looking inward, gauging her bodily responses. She wasn't panicked. Urgency, yes, she felt that, but also the same calm she usually felt before entering a field of action during an operation.

Could she trust that? She'd read accounts of soldiers with PTSD suffering paranoid delusions where they'd acted with calm certainty that they were the only ones who saw the danger clearly. Could she have fallen into that trap without even knowing it?

If she had—and dragged Megan down with her—it was even more reason to get off this island as quickly as possible. Bottom line: if she couldn't trust her judgment, she shouldn't be carrying a gun.

"Okay," Lucy finally said. "Here's what I see. They have Mateo's prints in Pastor Fleming's blood on the knife, a full palm print on a piece of paper with the safe combination, and on the insulin pump. That pretty much makes Mateo one of the world's most incompetent criminals, not even smart enough to wear gloves, so dumb he left the paper with his palm print and the safe combination there at the scene."

"Mateo's being framed—I've been telling you that all along."

"Right. But the real question is: by who? Who stands to gain most?"

"Mateo's family said it was a lot of cash—

Pastor Fleming was getting ready to pay people who'd made loans to third world ministries. Maybe he was trying to fake his death so he could steal the money but Mateo walked in on it?"

Cash loans funneled through a church? That needed looking into. Had all the makings of a Ponzi scheme. Lucy added it to her list. But first priority was getting Megan to safety.

"I still don't understand why we need to suddenly leave," Megan continued. "It'll take fifteen minutes to go grab our stuff from the hotel. How much danger could we be in if it was Pastor Fleming behind all this? He must be on the boat guarding Mateo, right?"

Good girl, filling in most of the blanks. Except the most important one. "When I was in Chief Hayden's office, she had a photo of her and Shelly Fleming. That's when I realized that I'd seen Chief Hayden in other photos—the Flemings' wedding pictures in their house. And family photos from when they were young. I think she's Shelly Fleming's sister. Or at the very least, a close friend."

"If the Chief of Police is involved, then we can't trust anyone." Megan shook her head. "I don't buy it. All those other police are also here—the sheriff's department and the crime scene techs from the state. The Coast Guard out searching for the boat."

"Except I don't think they are. I don't think she actually called anyone."

"There's one way to tell for sure. Let's go

back to the Flemings' house. You said yourself that crime scene would take days to process—that means the techs should still be there working."

It went against Lucy's instincts, but Megan had a point—there was little chance of anything happening, not in a public area. The most they'd lose would be some time. Still, if Megan hadn't made her stop and talk this out, they'd be halfway to the mainland by now.

"If there's no one there," Megan continued, "then you can call the state police yourself."

Except she couldn't. "I have no standing here and can't invite them into an investigation outside of their jurisdiction." Lucy sighed. "Best I can do is plant the idea. It will take hours, maybe days to find someone to listen and take action."

"Time Mateo doesn't have."

Lucy nodded, wishing she had a better answer for Megan. They sat in silence for a moment.

"I trust your instincts, Mom," Megan finally said. "But I can't just abandon Mateo and his family without concrete proof. And you'll need something to get the state police to take action. If there's no one at the Flemings, we can go—you can do what you need to do and I promise I'll wait in a hotel room or whatever, you won't need to worry about me."

Best deal Lucy was going to get. She started the car again and headed south toward the Fleming crime scene.

Chapter 17

MEGAN SAW THE way her mom's jaw clenched as she turned the car toward their hotel and the Flemings' house. Lucy was being paranoid—suspecting everyone and everything came with her job, sure, but even if Chief Hayden was involved, that didn't mean Megan and Lucy were in danger. In fact, it might mean the opposite.

"If the chief and Shelly are working with Pastor Fleming, then Mateo ruined their plan, right?" she said, trying out her theory. "So they're scrambling, trying to cover their tracks. There's no way they'd target us—it's too risky. They need us to back them up. In a way, we're their alibis. We're part of the story they're trying to sell."

Lucy's frown didn't ease. "If they feel desperate, backed into a corner, who knows what they might do."

"That's true of anyone. But Chief Hayden didn't seem desperate to me. And using Mateo in that video…" She thought for a moment. "Wait. Do you think the entire police force could be in on it?"

"You've been watching too many movies. My guess is that Plan A was to steal the money, make it look like a robbery gone bad leaving Fleming presumed dead—"

"Where'd all that blood come from?" Megan asked.

"Actually, the way it was spread out like that, it probably wasn't an extreme amount if you added it all up. It could have been diluted. Maybe Fleming was having his blood drawn and saving it up, who knows?"

"So it was all part of selling the idea that he was killed, his body taken?"

"Right. And Mateo was meant to find the crime scene, probably to establish a timeline where Shelly had an alibi."

"But Mateo showed up early."

"So they went with Plan B—setting Mateo up as a fall guy. Now they're trying to get even more money from Fleming's congregation while they're planting more evidence against Mateo."

"Wait." Megan felt her stomach squeeze tight as if someone was choking her. "Mom, for that to work—"

"They need to stage a scenario where they kill Mateo during a dramatic hostage rescue. The money will have mysteriously vanished and life will go back to normal for the Flemings."

"But not for Mateo or his family. We have to stop them."

Lucy glanced over at her. "We have no proof," she warned. "This is just a wild-assed theory. But it's the only theory I can make fit all the facts."

They were almost to the Flemings' house. This section of the island with the shopping center and marina was better lit than the residential area they'd just driven through. Despite the fact that it should have been a hub of activity, the Flemings' house was dark. There was crime scene tape strung across the gate and a police cruiser parked there, but no sign of a police officer.

"Damn," Lucy muttered. "That's it. We're leaving."

"Let's at least grab our stuff from the room. We're here already."

Lucy didn't answer, but instead of pulling into the hotel's drive, she turned into the shopping center parking lot entrance, made an immediate U-turn, and headed back out on the main road heading away from their hotel. Before Megan could protest, her phone rang. Unknown caller.

"Hello?"

"Is this Megan? It's Chief Hayden. Can I please speak with your mother?"

"Uh, sure. Hang on." Megan turned the speakerphone on and held it up to Lucy. "It's the chief."

"Hello, this is Lucy." Megan marveled at the

way her mom's voice sounded so natural. Was this the way she sounded when she went undercover?

"Lucy, hi again. I finally had a chance to get your statements but—"

"Oh, sorry. We were starving and Megan was so upset about Mateo and that tape. It's my fault. I never should have let her get so close to the family. Is there any word? Have you found them?"

"No. Shelly is trying to raise the ransom, but on a Sunday night, it's tough going. She's putting out a call to his friends and parishioners to help. And there's been no trace of the boat, nothing we can track."

"Is there anything I can do to help? Glad to call in some of my people, if you want."

"I think between the state and county guys we've got it covered. The sheriff is going to get their helicopter with the infrared radar up for us."

"Good idea. Listen, can you get our statements in the morning? I really should make sure Megan is okay. This whole thing has been so traumatic for her."

Megan rolled her eyes at that but Lucy didn't smile. If anything, she seemed more tense, increasing their speed. They were almost to the drawbridge leading off the island.

"That will be fine. If I'm not here in the morning, any of my officers will be glad to help. Take care."

"Good luck—call me sooner if anything happens, will you?"

"Of course." The chief hung up.

They approached the bridge. It was up. There were two cars waiting, their taillights bright against the night. Lucy slowed, keeping a generous distance between her and the other cars, at least four or five car lengths.

"There's no boat," she said as they finally came to a stop.

"What?"

"They raise the bridge for the tall boats, but there's no boat."

"Maybe it's already passed through."

A man left the little shack that controlled the bridge and approached the first car in line. A few minutes later it made a U-turn and headed their way. Lucy flashed her lights and the driver pulled up. She rolled down her window. "What's going on?"

"Bridge is broken. Cable snapped or something. They're getting someone out to fix it but not sure how long it's going to be."

"Thanks." Lucy waited for the car to pass before making her own U-turn. "I think I made a huge mistake. Do you have Walden's home number in your cell?"

Isaac Walden was Lucy's second in command back in Pittsburgh. "No. I can call Dad. He'll have it."

Lucy blew her breath out. "Your dad is not going to be happy. Yeah, call him."

Megan dialed. "Dad? Hi there! Mom wants to talk to you."

"Megan, how are you? Did something more

happen? I wanted to discuss—"

"Nick," Lucy interrupted, "we might have more trouble here than I originally thought. I need you to call Walden, have him call me on Megan's cell."

No answer.

"Nick?"

Megan glanced at the phone. "The call was dropped." She tried dialing again. Dead silence. "I had three bars, but now they're gone." She dialed another number. "Nothing."

Lucy glanced up through the windshield. "One cell tower for the entire island. Easy to control. Like the bridge." She turned the car onto a private drive on the ocean side of the island. The mansion in front of them had no lights on and no gate. The driveway was circular. Lucy pulled around so they were facing out and parked. "Okay, we're going to have to do this the hard way."

"What's that mean?" Megan asked, for the first time feeling frightened. Suddenly this all felt very, very real. Life and death real. Was this how her mom felt all the time when she was at work?

"It means... are you up for a game of hide and seek?"

CHAPTER 18

AS LUCY SCOUTED the house, she forced herself to shift her emotions aside, although what she really wanted to do was scream in frustration. This was her fault; she'd allowed Megan to steer her away from the immediate action she'd wanted to take and now it was too late.

"Hide and seek?" Megan said, following Lucy back to the Subaru's trunk. "What does that mean?"

"It means we're going to find a safe place for you to hide." Lucy opened the lockbox in the trunk and pulled out her Remington. "While I seek."

"Mom—"

"No. This is the time when you listen, do as I say, and stop asking questions." Lucy loaded the shotgun, intending to leave it with Megan. Then she thought twice and set it aside. Sometimes it was more dangerous being armed than not, even if Megan was an experienced marksman. "I made a mistake. More than one. And now there's no time left."

"All we have to do is wait them out. Dad will make sure someone comes looking for us. Plus, there are plenty of other people on this island—not like they can keep the bridge up forever."

Lucy gave a little shake of her head. "You're thinking like a civilian. Try thinking like a cop turned criminal, who instead of a million dollar payoff and their nice, cushy job, is suddenly forced to go into cleanup mode as they make their getaway."

Megan stiffened, making a shuddering noise of dismay as she sucked in her breath. "Mateo. Now they have to kill him. Destroy the evidence."

"I miscalculated. Should have found a way to play along, insinuate myself into the investigation. I don't know. But your safety comes first." Lucy grabbed spare ammo for her Glock.

"We need to find him." Megan frowned. "But how? Chief Hayden could be going after Mateo right now. Should we find a way to follow her?"

Lucy was still trying to sort out the logistics. The only part of her plan that was solid was the part where Megan stayed way the hell away from all of it. "See if you can access the house's Wi-Fi with your phone or my laptop. If I can reach Walden, I think I have a way to find Mateo."

Megan opened the door to the back seat and

began working while Lucy shrugged into her tactical vest and added the items she needed to its many pockets. Her hand hovered over the combat medic kit but instead she grabbed a spare magazine, an extra Maglite, zip ties, and her ASP baton. She needed to be able to move fast and quiet. Lucy stashed her night vision monocular in the front pocket of her vest where it would be close to hand. She wished she had proper tactical clothing instead of shorts and sneakers, but at least this time she was heading into action wearing shoes.

"If the plan was for Pastor Fleming to fake his own death, maybe he's in danger now as well. One less witness and they could collect his life insurance," Megan said. Not for the first time Lucy thought what a great criminal mastermind her daughter would make. "It could take years to have him declared dead otherwise."

"Already there. If it comes to it, I'm hoping I can turn him against Hayden and his wife, and anyone else involved. But finding him and Mateo comes first. They must have a meeting place—maybe an empty house with a dock or a camping spot or coordinates out at sea to meet the boat?"

"They know you'll come after them."

"That's what worries me. Stopping me isn't enough—they have no idea who I've already talked to, not to mention Mateo's family and the other local cops. Even if they frame Mateo for Fleming's death, how are they going to cover their tracks once they get the money?"

"I got into the guest Wi-Fi," Megan said.

"Want me to text Dad?"

"Let me get the ball rolling with Walden first." His number was in Lucy's email contact list. She used the voice over internet app to call him. "I need you to loop Taylor in and my husband on a conference call," she instructed after she explained the situation to him. Soon her screen was filled with Walden's always-serious face; her best computer tech, Taylor's impetuous grin; and Nick managing to look both relieved and worried at the same time. Her A-team.

Taylor made quick work of the data she gave him, finding a second insulin pump registered to Flemings' account with the manufacturer. It was always little things like applying for a rebate or warranty that tripped up most criminals.

"Taylor, can you get me a GPS reading on Fleming's insulin pump?"

"Not without a warrant—if you want it admissible."

"Don't care about that. Exigent circumstances—there's a kid's life at stake." Besides it wasn't her jurisdiction or her case, so evidentiary rules be damned. Except. "If it's something illegal that you'll be busted for, tell me what to do and let the trail come back to me."

His head was bowed over his keyboard and he was humming AC/DC—which meant good news. "No worries. Just give me a sec."

She didn't ask for any details that might get them both in legal hot water down the road. Instead, she turned her attention to Walden.

"Anything on Hayden I could use as leverage?"

"I can see why she might need money. Her husband died last year, leaving a ton of medical bills. Looks like the house is in foreclosure."

Broke public servant in the midst of all this wealth—including her own sister? Could explain why Hayden was desperate enough to go along with Shelly and Robert. More than protecting her sister, she was hoping for a way to protect the home she'd shared with her husband.

Primal forces, defending family and home. Might make Hayden dangerous.

"I need back up. Sheriff's department if they have boats or a helo available, if not, go with the Coast Guard. Hell, I'll take the Beach Patrol and a few lifeguards if they have any tactical training. I don't like going up against fellow cops alone, not when they know the playbook as well as I do."

"Then don't," Nick urged. "Stay with Megan, keep her safe."

"I will if Fleming is too far away, but if he's close by—and I suspect he is—then there's no time to wait. The only way for Hayden and the Flemings to get away clean is to kill Mateo."

"*If* Chief Hayden and Mrs. Fleming are involved," Walden, her resident devil's advocate cautioned. "You have no proof. It's not against the law for a police chief to not call in outside assistance to help with a case. She's perfectly within her rights. So unless Mrs. Fleming already filed a false insurance claim for the stolen money, neither she nor the chief have broken any laws as far as we know."

"Maybe not yet," Lucy said. "Let's make sure we find Mateo before they have a chance."

Walden nodded. "I'll get right on it."

Which left her and Nick alone.

"Megan, could you walk down to the mailbox and get us the exact address, please?" Lucy asked. Megan looked like she was going to balk at the request, but then nodded and left, giving Lucy a few moments of privacy with Nick.

"What's your plan?" he asked, not wasting any time on recriminations.

"This house has an security system sticker so we can't risk going inside, but it's a warm night so I'm going to set up Megan on the porch. She should be safe. I'll leave her my laptop. If anything happens, she can get word out to you."

He nodded but the worry lines around his eyes deepened. "You know the boy's probably already dead and Fleming is halfway to Cuba."

"Maybe, but I need to try." She glanced over her shoulder in the direction Megan took. "Megan would never forgive me if I didn't."

"You'll take her cell phone so we can track you?"

"Yes." Damn, she needed to check the battery level on the phone. "As long as I have juice and there's Wi-Fi nearby, I should be able to stay in contact. And I'll wait for backup if I can."

"Be careful. You're not just dealing with a conman with a blown caper. If you're right about Hayden, then you're dealing with a trained law enforcement officer who has a lot to lose."

"Like Walden said, technically Hayden hasn't committed any crime yet—at least none that we have any evidence for. I'm hoping that will keep her on the sidelines, playing cautious and thinking twice before she does something she can't undo. Which leaves just Fleming and maybe his wife to deal with."

He didn't look convinced. But Megan was back from her jog down the road. "This is number 43 Marshland Road."

"Got it." Nick's tone turned stern. "Megan you do what your mother tells you to, no argument. Okay?"

"Yes, sir. Don't worry about me. I'll be fine." Megan was trying to act brave and grownup for Nick, but if Lucy could see through her, she was certain Nick did as well. Damn, she wished he was here.

"We'll both be fine," Lucy said firmly.

Before Nick could respond, Taylor returned. "I found them!"

Chapter 19

Lucy settled Megan on a settee on the front porch of the mansion. She couldn't tell what color it was in the dark, but it sported the lovely, balanced lines, and classic design of a Southern plantation house, complete with twin staircases leading down from the columned porch.

"You've got water, blanket, rations if you dare to eat them—they taste like sawdust—and the laptop has almost a full charge, so as long as you don't use it for anything else, you should be able to stay in contact with Dad."

"I already turned on the messenger app—it will take up tons less power than video conferencing and be just as fast. Plus you can message me from my phone."

Okay, learn something new everyday.

"I'll be fine," Megan said. "Go save Mateo."

Lucy hesitated. The tide was coming in. She could hear the waves growing louder from the back of the house. There were no lights to be seen, she'd be leaving Megan alone in the dark. Vulnerable. And she hated that.

"Maybe I should stay. Let the sheriff handle things."

"No. Mom, do your job. Please."

Still, Lucy had doubts. Should she change her mind and leave the Remington with Megan? No. Odds were the next people Megan saw would be law enforcement: either Hayden's men filled with Lord only knew what tall tales the chief had spun for them or a sheriff department's hyped-up emergency response team. Last thing she wanted to risk was trusting them to think first and shoot second if Megan made the wrong move with the shotgun.

No. This was the best way, the safest way. And the hardest damn way.

Megan got up, the blanket still wrapped around her, and threw her arms around Lucy. "Thanks, Mom."

"For what?"

"For believing in me. For trusting my instincts about Mateo. For treating me like an adult."

Was that what she was doing? She squeezed Megan back. Didn't mention that if she was wrong about all this, if Fleming really was the victim and Mateo their actor, then she'd be the one destroying Mateo's future.

Except... she did trust Megan's instincts. And her own. Ever since her injury, fighting back physically and mentally, she'd been second-guessing every choice. But not now. Now she was certain she was right.

She kissed Megan's forehead—would have kissed the top of her head like she did when Megan was little, submerging herself in the perfume of baby shampoo and innocence, but Megan had grown too tall for that.

"I'll see you soon," she promised. "Everything will be all right."

A double promise. Tempting Fate. But for once, Lucy didn't care. The confidence of knowing she was right and that she'd keep her word surged through her.

Lucy let Megan go and turned, jogged down the steps, barely feeling the thud of pain echoing through her bad ankle. Everything was going to be all right—because she was going to make sure of it.

She sped off in the Subaru, watching Megan in the rearview, a tiny shadow draped in deeper shadows of the house and the moonless night. For the first time in longer than she could remember, she didn't feel a pang of regret or fear by letting her daughter out of her sight.

Megan would be fine. She was a smart girl—no, not a girl, not any more. A smart young woman. Brave and strong and she had her father's intuition about people and her mother's pig-headed stubborn refusal to give up and her own savvy, sly instincts that combined the two.

Lucy smiled. God help anyone who dared to go up against her daughter. Megan's black belt would be the least of their worries.

"DON'T TELL ME you're getting squeamish now," a woman's voice pierced the haze surrounding Mateo. He couldn't stay awake; the drugs were still messing with his mind. They'd returned him to the boat's storage compartment, a wide cupboard with a door that opened out. He tried kicking at the door but his legs were asleep and he couldn't pull them back far enough to get any leverage. At least he'd been able to see that Pastor Fleming was still alive.

They had to get out of here, soon. Pastor Fleming had looked awful. He wasn't going to last much longer.

"When you called me for help, it didn't include murder," a second woman answered. They were moving about up on the deck, making the boat shimmy and shake.

"It's not murder if it's natural causes. Diabetic ketoacidosis. That's what the autopsy will show."

Mateo froze. They were talking about killing Pastor Fleming. Funny, part of him had imagined that the man he'd heard earlier was Pastor Fleming—that he was the one who'd given Mateo the drugs and dragged him onto the boat. He still wasn't sure how he'd been drugged; he remembered a glass of iced tea and nothing after that, but even that memory was foggy. Was that iced tea something he'd drunk with Megan? Or maybe with his family during lunch? Time was all confused. It was like looking through a crazy kaleidoscope, hard to tell what was real with so many fragments that didn't fit together.

"I'm not talking about Robert and you know it."

"Kid's own damn fault, meddling where he had no business."

There was a pause and the sound of something heavy being dropped with a thud. A body? Was Mateo next? He squirmed, trying to push against the cupboard door.

"Tell me one thing. Robert faking his death, that was his plan. Was killing him yours from the beginning?"

"Fool expected me to wait until the courts declared him dead so I could collect the life insurance. While he took the money and ran. This way I get it all—"

"Except you're not. Can't you see how wrong it's all gone? Technically, you haven't broken any laws since it was Robert who took Mateo. Let me call it in. We'll be the heroes."

Pastor Fleming had brought Mateo here? Impossible—or was it? Mateo strained to remember, but the only thing he was certain of was the blood he'd found at Pastor Fleming's house.

"And the money?" The first woman's voice had turned sharp, demanding. It was tantalizingly familiar but between the drugs and the way the voices were distorted by the wall separating Mateo from the women, he couldn't place it. "I'm giving you a lifeline, your chance to save your home, clear all the debt Jack's illness racked up. But what's in it for me?"

"I don't care about any damn money. We need to stop this before it goes too far. While I can still salvage my career and you can stay out of prison."

"No." The other woman's voice was determined. Mateo felt as if a death sentence had just been passed. "The kid's seen too much. And if Robert lives, he'll figure out that I swapped his insulin for water. He loves me but not enough to forgive me for trying to kill him. We need to get rid of them both. Tonight."

Chapter 20

"FLEMING'S PUMP IS at the nature preserve on the west side of the island. According to the satellite maps," Taylor told Lucy as she drove toward the location. "The reason why that area is uninhabited is because it's basically a maze of inlets and tidal marshes. Perfect place for a boat to hide."

"And faster for a boat to flee from, disappear into another section of the marsh or vanish out to sea."

"Especially Fleming's boat. Only has a fourteen inch draft, so the tide's not much of an issue."

Damn. Could nothing go right tonight?

"How long for the sheriff's men?"

"They're about forty minutes out."

The sign for the nature preserve appeared on her right. She slowed and turned into the parking lot. There were two other vehicles already there: Shelly Fleming's and Chief Hayden's. "I'm here now."

No answer. Lucy glanced at the phone. No Wi-Fi signal here in the nature preserve and the cell tower was still down. Guess she was going it alone.

She grabbed her Remington and left the car. On the other side of the parking lot, there was movement in the tall grass leading out to the marsh. She aimed her flashlight just in time to spot an alligator slipping through the grass.

Great. One more thing to worry about. But she was more concerned about the human predators than the reptilian ones. A map at the end of the parking lot revealed several trails braided through the preserve. One of them twisted around the inlet where Fleming's boat was anchored. She'd have to go cross-country for the final approach, but it would get her close.

She swapped her flashlight for her thermal night vision monocular, scouting the trail ahead. It was amazing how much more detail the monocular could pick up than her own vision even aided by a flashlight. The trail she'd chosen was narrow, maybe four feet wide, with thick foliage on either side, including knee-high, sharp-leafed palmettos that sliced at her bare legs. Crowded pine trees and gnarled live oaks, Spanish moss dangling from their limbs, created a claustrophobic atmosphere. It didn't help that the sulfur smell of decay overrode the more pleasant scent of the pine needles that cushioned the hard-packed surface of the trail.

The forest wasn't quiet; instead, it was filled with random noises ambushing her from every side. Squawks of birds or maybe frogs, deep-throated notes that came from frogs or maybe insects, splashes that Lucy hoped were fish or birds and not alligators.

She was using her monocular when sudden movement sparked through the thermal sensors. Something darted from the brush and stopped on the path. It was a strangely shaped image—too short to be a gator. It turned to face her. An armadillo, complete with prehistoric armor, blinked at her. Then it scurried away, the plants rustling behind it.

She kept moving. The trail twisted around a lagoon that gave a hint of the wider stretch of water beyond, then a boardwalk appeared. According to the map at the trailhead, the boardwalk headed in the direction she wanted to go, so she moved across it. The stench grew worse as she walked above the marsh. The clicking noises of crabs scurrying across the mud below made her wonder if the tide was low enough for her to cross through the mud, sneak up on the boat. When she turned to scan the area between the boardwalk and the sound, she could make out several birds walking over the mud and caught sight of another alligator as it slinked along the bank.

One more curve and the tree branches thinned enough for her to see the boat. It was at anchor in an inlet surrounded by trees and mud on three sides. A few tiny slits of light were all that made it through the cabin windows—black-out curtains, she guessed. Thick grass rippled in the night breeze, making it appear as if the boat were moored in the middle of a hay field. She was tempted to climb over the boardwalk's railing and simply walk up to the boat.

No way it would be that easy. Movement caught her eye as an alligator she hadn't spotted before glided past, following an unseen current through what had appeared to be solid ground. Swamp. That's what this was.

Okay, so how did Hayden and Shelly Fleming get to the boat? Lucy continued on the boardwalk, moving slower and bending low to keep out of sight. A cluster of trees got in the way, but then the boat came into view once more, only twenty feet or so away from the boardwalk.

A Zodiac type of motorized raft was lashed to the railing at the stern. Question answered. She judged her options. The boardwalk continued on but turned inland, away from the boat. She made out several heat signatures in the boat's cabin but they were so close together it was difficult to be certain how many there were. Four, she hoped, because that would mean Mateo was still alive.

Several sprawling limbs from a live oak reached out toward the boat, one stretched over the raft. She eyed the tree. Its trunk emerged from the mud a good three feet from the boardwalk. Lucy mapped it out in her mind: climb the railing, leap onto the trunk, shimmy up to the branch, then over the branch to the raft, lower herself down…

No sweat if she were ten years younger and didn't have a bum ankle to worry about.

The boat began to rock. Light speared the night as the cabin door opened. Two figures emerged, one carrying a large duffle. Lucy couldn't make out their faces, not at this distance, but they definitely were both women.

She focused her monocular on the cabin. Now the two heat sources left behind were easier to make out. Both were low, on the deck, but not spread out like they were lying down, rather balled up and not moving. Restrained? Perhaps shoved into a compartment? She hadn't had a chance to view any plans for Fleming's cabin cruiser, but the ransom video made it look a lot like the inside of a RV or camper.

If the two heat sources were Fleming and Mateo, why would they both be restrained? Why wasn't Fleming up and about if he was the mastermind?

Had Lucy gotten this all wrong?

CHAPTER 21

FOR ONCE, MEGAN didn't mind being left behind while Lucy went to work. She wasn't even resentful that she'd been relegated to the sidelines. And for the first time in a long time, she wasn't worried about her mom.

Something had broken inside her mother a few months ago when she was injured. Megan had diagnosed PTSD and a reactive depression—from the way her dad acted around Lucy, she guessed he agreed. But today, Lucy was back, the confident posture, the quick thinking, piecing together almost invisible clues to come up with the answer while everyone else was still figuring out the right question to ask.

She smiled and pulled the fleece blanket tighter around her. Definitely warmer than Pittsburgh, but the wind was coming right at her here at the front of the house. After a few moments of shivering, she got to her feet, gathered the laptop and water bottle, left the package of rations, and strolled to the back of the house. Definitely less windy here.

The back yard was fenced in with gates at the drive where Megan stood and at the path leading out to the dunes—probably because it had a pool and spa. Wouldn't want anyone wandering off the beach falling in.

She raised the latch and walked past the pool to the deck area beside the rear wall of the house. There were chairs and chaise lounges scattered around and the area was sheltered above by the overhang of the upper deck, making it much warmer than the front porch. She curled up on a lounge chair, set up the laptop on a table beside her, and snuggled under the blanket. The sound of the waves was hypnotic and there was something in the salt air that made her drowsy.

That was the problem with waiting; it was so damned boring. She leaned back, not fighting the feeling—if Dad or Mom texted the computer would alarm—and allowed her eyes to drift shut.

"Hands where I can see them," a man's voice sliced through the gentle sound of the surf like a cleaver.

Megan blinked as a bright light speared her vision. She couldn't make out the man behind the light.

"Hands," he repeated.

She slowly slid her hands out from under the

blanket, holding them palms forward so he could see they were empty.

"Megan, is that you?" The light inched down just enough for her to make out Officer Gant's face. "Where's your mother? What are you doing here?"

Gant. Chief Hayden's right hand man. Panic sizzled through Megan although she fought not to show it. Stay calm. Focus. That's what Lucy would do. "How did you find me?"

"There's an alarm on the swimming pool gate."

Shit. Megan didn't hold her breath—that was the worst thing to do if you might be getting ready to fight or make a run for it. Instead, she planted her feet firmly, moved the blanket aside so she wouldn't get tangled in it, and scanned the area for possible weapons.

Nothing within reach except her laptop. Ahh... the best weapon of all. She twisted her body to face Gant, brushing her arm against the keyboard to wake the sleeping computer. Two clicks, that's all she needed, just time enough for two clicks and she could activate the video chat app.

"Why are you here?" Gant asked taking one step toward her and stopping as if she posed a threat. "Where's your mother?"

How much did he know? Was he in on it, working with Chief Hayden? Or just an innocent cop caught up in the chief's web of lies?

"Thought you'd be working with the sheriff and state lab people over at the Fleming's house," she said.

He shifted his weight as if uncomfortable. Ah-hah, Megan thought. He knows. And he knows we know. Was that good or bad? If he was working with the Flemings and Hayden did he now realize he'd have to silence Megan as well? She just needed to distract him, two seconds, that's all she needed. But how?

He ignored her implied accusation to glance over his shoulder, his hand falling to his weapon. "Answer me, Megan. Where's your mother?"

Megan jerked her chin toward the drive at his back. Gant's gaze followed as he drew his gun. She darted her hand out to the computer and clicked. Gant caught the movement and whirled back.

"Stop. Don't move," he ordered. Megan froze, her hand in mid-air.

The computer made the pinging sound of the video connection and Taylor's face appeared. "Megan. What's up?" he asked, squinting at the screen.

"There's a police officer named Gant here," she said, somehow managing to keep her words from tumbling over each other in her rush of relief. "He has his gun drawn and is asking about my mother."

Gant holstered his gun and approached. "Who the hell is that?"

"That," Megan told him, "is the FBI."

"Special Agent Taylor. We've been fully briefed and the sheriff's department and state police are on their way. Step back from Ms. Callahan,

Officer Gant."

"The FBI? Why—someone want to fill me in on what the hell is going on?" Gant asked, his gaze swiveling from Megan to Taylor's face on the screen to checking the area behind him as if expecting an ambush.

"Does this have something to do with Chief Hayden cancelling the crime scene unit?" He lowered his light so they could now look each other in the eye. "It wasn't just budgetary concerns, was it?"

"Did you ever call the sheriff for help?" Megan asked.

His lips tightened and she was sure he was going to tell her it was none of her business or ask what right a kid had to be questioning a cop's authority. But Gant surprised her. "I did. Found out later the chief cancelled them as well."

"Like she also shut down the cell tower and left the drawbridge up so no one could leave Harbinger Cove?"

He pulled out his cell phone with his other hand—meaning he wasn't about to shoot her, Megan noted with relief. "Did Chief Hayden send you here to hurt my mother? Stop her from talking?"

Confusion crossed his features before he blanked them. "Why would the chief—talking about what?"

"About how that crime scene was staged by Pastor Fleming. About how he was faking his own death, and how he kidnapped Mateo to frame him, or how the chief and Mrs. Fleming are helping to cover it all up."

"Megan—" Taylor's voice cut through hers, a warning. Right, never give away too much. But he wasn't the one here with a guy three times her size carrying a gun.

Gant must have had his doubts already. Or he'd seen enough behind the scenes to put it all together as well. Because his shoulders sagged and he blew his breath out as if surrendering. "It was those damn church loans, wasn't it? I knew it was too good to be true, but the chief put her own money in and Fleming was her brother-in-law—"

"Do you know where the chief is now?" Taylor asked.

Gant shook his head. "She left me to cover any calls, said she was going to inspect the crime scene again."

"There was no one there when we drove by," Megan said. "Just an empty patrol car."

"She's probably with Fleming and her sister," Taylor said. "The sheriff's emergency response team is still half an hour out."

"You found Fleming's boat?" Gant asked.

"My mom's on her way there now."

"She left you here alone?"

"Thought I'd be safe from the chief and any cops working with her. I would have been if I stayed out front where I was supposed to."

"She had the right idea. Stay here and I'll go watch your mom's back. Tell me where she is."

Megan wanted to go with him, make sure her

mom was okay. But she realized she was a liability—not because she was a kid or because she couldn't handle herself in a crisis. Because if things went wrong, she could be used as a hostage against her mother.

And the fact that Gant wanted her to stay behind proved that he was one of the good guys. Didn't it?

She glanced at Taylor. He looked uncertain as well.

"If the chief's there already, Lucy will need back up," Gant said, obviously impatient. "If I was in on it, I'd already know where they are, wouldn't I?"

"Unless they doubled crossed you and left, taking the money," Megan argued.

"Your choice. You want your mom outnumbered three-to-one or you want to trust me?"

Megan scrutinized him and decided to do what Lucy would do: trust her gut. "Tell him," she instructed Taylor.

Taylor nodded his agreement and the screen switched to a map with the GPS location flagged.

"Skeleton Marsh," Gant said.

"Skeleton Marsh?" Megan echoed, not liking the sound of that.

"Yep. Got its name because it's where pirates used to dump bodies—between the crabs and the alligators, if you ever found anything left, it was only bits and pieces of—"

"Their skeleton. How far is it?"

"Ten minutes." He hesitated. "Are you okay here?"

"I'll stay with her," Taylor said. "And inform the sheriff and state police that you'll also be on the scene." It was a thinly veiled warning but Gant simply jerked his chin in a nod, turned, and jogged back to his car.

The night grew silent once more, even the hypnotic pounding of the surf seemed muted. Megan took a deep breath and sat down with the computer.

"Thanks, Taylor."

"You're welcome. I'm texting your mom to let her know Gant is on the way and I'll update your dad and Walden. Be back in a jiff."

Nothing to do now but wait. And Megan was quickly learning waiting was the hardest job of all.

Chapter 22

LUCY WATCHED AS the woman with the duffle threw it onto the raft tied to the rear of Fleming's boat. The second woman stood back, keeping guard on the men in the cabin, a pistol in her hand. "We should leave now. That FBI agent—" she said. Chief Hayden.

Which made the other woman Shelly Fleming. "That FBI agent has nothing on us. Especially not after she finds Mateo Romero killed himself rather than go to jail for the rest of his life." She shook her head. "Poor baby. So upset after accidentally killing the sweet, kindly Pastor Fleming when he took him hostage and didn't get him his insulin. Leaving me a grieving but soon-to-be rich widow and you, big sis, still Chief of Police. Although I can't for the life of me understand why that matters so much to you."

They were still talking as they moved inside, out of hearing range. Lucy checked Megan's phone. Still no cell signal and no Wi-Fi in range. She returned the phone to the vest's watertight inside pocket where it would stay safe.

She needed both hands to make it over to the boat, so she left the Remington behind as she climbed onto the railing. The tree seemed farther away than she thought, but she'd learned as a kid that climbing trees was more about attitude than technique. She flung herself out over the mud and grabbed hold of the tree trunk. The bark wasn't as brittle as the oaks back home, lots of small gnarled bits to dig in with her hands and feet. It scratched at her bare legs and arms, but soon, she was edging along a twisted limb, admiring the live oak's structure. Definitely a good climbing tree.

Despite her messed-up ankle, which made her second guess every other step as she planted that foot, she made it across the branch, over the mudflat and to the Zodiac in only a few minutes. The night noises of the wildlife in the marsh covered her movements nicely. The boat rocked gently as small waves lapped against it. Tide coming in.

She swung down over the Zodiac, weight suspended by her hands, and dropped the few feet down into it. Her landing made a thudding noise like a rock thrown into a pond. She flattened herself against the bottom of the boat, waiting for a response but none came.

Okay, stage one complete. Now for the hard

part. She had to assume both women were armed and she knew Hayden was also trained. Even if she surprised them inside the cabin, she'd still be outnumbered and all they had to do to negate Lucy's efforts would be to threaten the hostages.

How to get them away from their captives?

She sat up and pulled the duffle bag toward her. Heavy. At least twenty pounds. She opened it. Wads of cash banded together. Close to a million, she guessed given the weight and dimensions.

A gator slid past the raft, its tail swishing the mud and water into a murky, silt-laden wake. Lucy thought for a moment. She didn't have to get the hostages safe to shore; all she needed was to buy some time until the sheriff's department arrived.

She untied the line anchoring the raft to the boat. With the tide coming in, the current pushed her inland, deeper into the lagoon and mud.

Once she was halfway between the boardwalk and the boat, she grabbed her Maglite and secured it to the side of the raft where it would shine out over the mud between her and the boat. Then she grabbed a few handfuls of cash.

"Mrs. Fleming?" she called out in a neighborly yoo-hoo shout. "Think I found something that belongs to you!"

Light flooded the boat deck as the cabin door banged open. Shelly ran to the railing, followed by Hayden.

"I'll trade you," Lucy said. She tossed a bunch of bills into the air. They fluttered on the night breeze then landed on the mud where the crabs skittered toward them, seeking food.

"Are you crazy?" Shelly screamed. "What the hell are you doing?" She raised a pistol and aimed it at Lucy.

"If I go down, so does your money," Lucy called back. "Explain it to her, Chief. Simple hostage exchange. The money for Mateo and Fleming." She hoped Fleming was still alive—given what Shelly said a few minutes ago, it might already be too late for the pastor.

"Shoot her, Norah," Shelly urged her sister. "We'll get the money back and leave her to the gators."

"She's wearing a bulletproof vest," Hayden said, although she did raise her weapon and point it at Lucy. "No way can I make a head shot, not with that light in my eyes."

"So shoot the light," Shelly said.

"Or I could shoot you," Lucy replied, aiming her Glock. "Now that you've threatened a federal agent, I'd be justified."

"We haven't done anything," Shelly yelled back. "We're the heroes here. We found all this, were moving that cash to keep it safe from my husband. He's the bad guy here, not us."

"Then toss your weapons overboard. I'm sure you ladies won't mind waiting out there where I can keep an eye on you. The sheriff's department is on its way."

As if on cue, a speedboat appeared at the lagoon's outlet. At first, Lucy was relieved; this would be over and done with in a few minutes. But then she realized that the boat was a civilian one, similar to the flat-bottomed outboard Mateo's uncle had used to rescue her earlier. And there was only one man in it, not the SWAT team she'd been expecting.

Gant.

Chapter 23

SHELLY SPOTTED GANT'S boat about the same time as Lucy but her reaction surprised Lucy. Shelly whirled, raised her pistol, and aimed it at her older sister. "You bitch, you sold me out!"

Hayden raised her own weapon but it was clear she didn't have the heart to shoot her little sister. "Shelly, no. It's over. Drop your gun."

Gant revved his engine faster at the sight of a gun trained on his chief while Lucy grabbed the paddle and pushed-pulled the raft through the thick silt, aiming for the dive platform at the rear of the boat where she could climb on board.

As Gant roared into the protected water of the lagoon, the wake churned the mud and rocked the larger boat and Lucy's raft, pushing Lucy back, maddeningly just out of reach.

Above her, silhouetted in the light of the

open cabin door and Lucy's Maglite, Hayden lunged for her sister. A gunshot sounded above the growl of Gant's outboard. Lucy stopped paddling and risked standing, bracing herself against the side of the raft as the wake from Gant's boat rocked it. She raised her pistol and aimed at the two women struggling on the deck. She was still a good six feet away from being able to board the boat, but close enough to shoot, if need be.

Shelly pushed Hayden back, hard, and Hayden flew over the railing on the opposite side of the boat from Lucy's position.

Shelly straightened, holding a pistol. Gant shouted something but his words were buried in the noise of the outboard. He slowed, throttled down the engine to idle, drew a weapon, and stood.

"Drop the gun, Shelly!" Gant shouted. Shelly fired twice at him. He returned fire as did Lucy, but the rocking raft and aiming up at a moving target, all she hit was the side of the boat. Shelly vanished. Lucy wasn't sure if Gant hit her or if she'd dropped to the deck for cover.

She glanced past the stern of the boat to Gant's boat. He was slumped against the tiller, the boat pivoting in response, speeding up and aiming past Fleming's boat, directly at her raft. The outboard whined as it revved up, fighting the mud and silt, bouncing once as it hit something—Lucy prayed it was a log or alligator or anything except Hayden who she had lost sight of once she went overboard.

The impact sent Gant reeling over the side,

leaving the outboard racing out of control. It skimmed past the stern of Fleming's boat and rammed the Zodiac, flinging the lighter raft into the air and upending it. Lucy half dove, half flew into the water, aiming away from the outboard's propeller.

Except it wasn't really water—it was a thick goo, more like quicksand than anything. Gant's boat crashed into the boardwalk behind her, the Zodiac spun to a stop, turned upside down—the bag of money vanished into the mud and her Maglite gone with it, leaving her flailing, gasping, with only the light from Fleming's boat cabin to orient herself.

The mud sucked her under before she had a chance to hold her breath. A nasty taste filled her mouth and she panicked for a moment as waves churned the water above her.

Calm, focus, Nick's voice came in the dark. The memory of watching the crabs skitter over the mud and the alligator glide through it flashed through her. She stopped kicking, realizing that was only making things worse. The mud caught her feet, dragging her down.

She straightened, pulling her head above the water and hauled in a breath. It was like quicksand, she thought. The impact of the outboard crashing into the raft had left her only a few feet from Fleming's boat. Spitting the foul grit from her mouth she performed a slow-motion combination of wading and swimming. The mud fought her, sucking greedily at her feet, taking her shoes, but bare feet were the least of her worries. Thankfully, she'd kept hold of her gun, but she needed to eliminate the threat that was Shelly and then find Gant and Hayden.

Her ears were clogged with mud but she heard splashing from the opposite side of the boat. Either Gant or Hayden—hopefully both—still alive. Above her Shelly was slamming around in the cabin, swearing, obviously unharmed.

Just as Lucy reached the small dive platform to the side of the large outboard engine, the engine gave a cough and sputter. Fearful of the propeller, Lucy quickly hauled herself up onto the platform, landing not with the tactical posture she'd hoped for but more like a muddy whale beaching itself. From inside the cabin, Shelly shouted a curse and the engine roared to life in response.

The boat lurched forward then jerked to a stop again, the engine whining then quieting to a fretful gasping noise. Shelly had forgotten about the anchors. Lucy grabbed hold of the railing and climbed to her feet, one hand holding her gun. She edged forward onto the main deck toward the open cabin door.

Shelly was at the wheel, fighting the throttle, her hair in a tangled frenzy as she cried in frustration.

"It's over," Lucy said. No sign of Shelly's gun, but she wasn't taking any chances. She planted her feet and aimed. "Hands in the air where I can see them."

Shelly spun around. Her hands were empty,

which was the only thing that saved Lucy from shooting her.

"It's not my fault," she whimpered. "It wasn't supposed to happen like this."

"Turn the engine off," Lucy ordered.

Shelly nodded, tears and mascara streaming down her face, and shut the engine off. Lucy moved forward, but she knew she'd won. Shelly didn't resist as Lucy put her face down on the deck and restrained her with a set of zipcuffs.

A banging coming from a cabinet inside the cabin door grabbed her attention. Holding her pistol at the ready, she opened it. Mateo rolled out, his hands cuffed behind him.

"Pastor Fleming," he gasped. "You have to help him. He's dying."

Lucy opened the door to the bathroom. Fleming was on the floor, curled around the toilet, his color ashen and his breathing coming hard and fast, smelling sweet.

The boat rocked abruptly. Lucy whirled to face the new threat, but it was Gant at the diver's platform. "A little help here?"

He hauled Hayden's still form with him through the mud. As Lucy rushed to help them both on board, the sound of new, louder, powerful engines thundered through the night. Blinding spotlights pierced the darkness.

"Sheriff's department!" a man's voice sounded, amplified by a bullhorn.

Lucy couldn't stop her laughter, mud streaming down her clothing, inside and out, sliding from her hair into her face. Better late than never.

Chapter 24

THE SHERIFF'S DEPARTMENT had a tactical medic with them who quickly got Fleming stabilized, staunched the bleeding from the gash in Hayden's head where she'd hit it going overboard, and dispatched them along with Mateo to the hospital on the mainland while his colleagues ferried Shelly, Lucy, and Gant ashore. Gant had been hit in his vest, which was why he'd lost control of his boat, but refused to leave for the hospital until the others were taken care of.

Lucy and Gant were relegated to the back of a deputy's cruiser, which would need a serious hosing down to get the dead-fish pluff mud stink out of it. The mud had slipped and slid into every crevice of Lucy's clothing, making a squishing noise each time she shifted her weight.

"I can't believe—the chief," Gant said. "We've worked together for almost a decade."

"When did her sister move here?"

"Three years ago. Should've seen through his Ponzi scheme, but they were always so good about paying folks back. We all thought we were doing something good—helping others. So we kept on reinvesting."

"He paid the first ones in with the new money and that whet your appetite, until—"

"Until it all fell apart." He made a small noise. "Do you think the chief was she in on it the whole time?"

As if being a FBI agent gave Lucy special psychic powers. She thought of the way Shelly ordered Hayden around on the boat and how Hayden hesitated, balked each step of the way. "No. If she'd have known earlier, she would have paid off her debts after her husband died. I think she was just as surprised as anyone when she saw the blood at her sister's house. But after, when things went wrong, I think that's when Shelly realized she couldn't finish it alone. She convinced Hayden to help."

"Family." The word emerged with a sigh. "Hard to resist."

They sat in silence for a while. It was strange being in the back of a patrol car—the seat was hard plastic, not comfortable at all. And she didn't like the claustrophobic feeling of being confined. Of course, that was the entire point of the design.

"So your daughter, she's how old again?" Gant finally said.

"Fourteen. Why?"

"Pretty smart for a teenager, putting this all together." He glanced over at her, weighing his words. "She insisted I listen, was a bit of a—"

"Stubborn?" Lucy supplied when he stopped short of using a term men had used to label her through her entire professional career.

He jerked his chin in a nod. "Yeah. Definitely stubborn. Ferocious even."

Lucy smiled. Another adjective often applied to her by other law enforcement officers—not always as a compliment. "She gets that from her mother."

AT THE ER, the nurses quickly realized that if they were going to adequately assess Lucy for any injuries—she had none, but they wouldn't take the word of a civilian—they'd need to allow her to shower first. Which was just fine with her. It felt so good getting all the goo out of her hair and sluiced from her body. When she emerged, the nurses had taken all her dirty clothes but left her a clean pair of scrubs and a bag with all her belongings.

Feeling like a refugee, barefoot and soaking wet, Lucy limped down the hall to the waiting area, her ankle screaming for mercy.

Screams that were immediately stifled when she saw Megan waiting for her. She rushed to hug her tight. "Are you all right?"

The question was a mother's reflex. Megan laughed, tears slipping down her cheeks. "Me?

You're the one who went swimming with gators."

Neither of them mentioned the humans armed with guns—mundane danger compared to alligators.

"Is Mateo okay?" Lucy asked. The nurses wouldn't tell her anything, FBI agent or not. And none of Mateo's family were in the waiting room, which could be a good sign or a bad one.

"He's fine. They said he was drugged with ketamine. He's a bit dehydrated, they want to watch him overnight. The pastor's really sick, but they said he'll make it. And Chief Hayden is in surgery, something about a brain injury and swelling. I'm not sure about her."

Lucy didn't have much sympathy for the chief. She understood about putting your family first, but Hayden had also sworn to protect and serve innocents like Mateo.

"Gant told me what you did, deciding to trust him, sending him to help."

Megan looked up, a guarded expression on her face. "I had to decide if he was one of the good guys or not—had to trust my gut since I didn't have anything else to go on." She blew her breath out, her shoulders sagging. "It was hard, Mom. Really, really hard. If I was wrong, he could have killed you."

Could have killed Megan as well. Lucy squeezed her tighter. "You did good. I'm proud of you."

They separated and Megan nodded to the plastic bag in Lucy's hand. "Is my phone in there?

Hope it's okay because Dad said to call him."

As Lucy fished in the bag for the phone, Megan pulled her down the hall. "Mateo and his family wan to see you, say thanks."

Despite Lucy's slow, stumbling gait—she was half tempted to borrow a cane from the ER—Megan practically danced beside her, obviously still high on adrenaline.

"You know," Megan continued, "Officer Gant said they'd need a new police chief after all this. Said you'd be perfect for the job."

Ahh… was this what had Megan so excited? "Would you want to move here, so far away from your friends?"

Megan considered it. "No. I mean, it's nice here and all, but I'd be bored. And Chief Hayden seemed like she worked like all the time—I want you to spend more time with me and Dad, not less. Besides, if you were chief in a small town like this, all the kids would know it—it'd be worse then you sending me to a convent!"

Lucy stifled her chuckle. "Maybe that wouldn't be a bad thing."

"Yeah, right. But seriously, Mom, I know you're not happy with the way your job is now. You can't let the FBI keep you behind a desk—it's making you miserable."

"You'd want to stay in Pittsburgh, right?" They pretty much had to with Nick's job. "That'd be okay with you?"

"Sure. My friends are all there and my soccer team and I like my school. Wait. Did you find a job somewhere else? You didn't turn it down just because of me?"

Oh, to be fourteen and have the world revolve around you. Lucy stopped and smiled at her daughter. She reached a hand to tame one of Megan's wayward curls.

"I would have, if it came to that. Your and Dad's happiness mean more to me than any job." It hurt to say the words; Lucy had always believed her job was who she was, not just what she did. But she finally understood—Hayden was wrong. She'd thought it had to be either/or, family or protect and serve the community who trusted her with their lives.

There were other ways to serve. And she didn't have to carry a badge to do it. But before she could devote herself to anyone else, she needed to take care of herself and her family.

"I have a few options. We'll talk more when we get home," she told Megan. "But you're right. I'm miserable behind a desk. It's time to leave the FBI and move on."

Megan nodded with a wisdom greater than her years. "I think you're doing the right thing. Remember what Grams always said, every new beginning is the start of a new adventure."

They arrived at Mateo's room. It was filled with the joyful noise of family. A nurse emerged, shaking her head at the crowd inside. "Go on in. What's one more?"

As soon as they crossed into the room, both Megan and Lucy were immediately embraced, working their way through a sea of smiling faces until they reached Mateo's bedside. His color was back to normal already, thanks to the IV in his arm, Lucy guessed.

"Lucy! Megan!" His grin was wide and Lucy wondered if he was still feeling the effects of the ketamine. "I'm so glad you're here. My heroes."

Megan laughed, grabbing onto his arm, blushing. "All in a day's work for my mom."

Pride burned through Lucy at Megan's praise. It had been so very long since Megan had anything nice to say about Lucy or her job she'd almost forgotten how good it felt.

"They say I can go home tomorrow. Can I still give you surfing lessons? It's the least I can do—and I promise, no more standing you up."

They both looked at Lucy, waiting for her answer. As if there were any way she could say no. "Sure."

Megan grabbed Lucy's free arm. "Thanks, Mom!" Then she sobered. "Are you sure you're going to be all right?" she asked Mateo. "We don't have to surf. We can just walk on the beach and you can teach me more about the architecture and history."

Lucy blinked. When had her daughter learned how to flirt so effortlessly?

"Do you remember anything?" she asked Mateo.

"No." He frowned. "Just blood. All that blood. Where did it come from?"

"My guess is Pastor Fleming. Wouldn't be

hard for him or his wife to get a hold of some medical supplies," she eyed Mateo's IV tubing, "take a little every week or so, then when they're ready, spray it around to fake their crime scene."

Jorge winced while Mateo's mother and aunt made small noises of dismay. Megan frowned at Lucy for ruining the moment—back to being the mom who couldn't get anything right.

Megan's phone rang. Nick. A little silt and mud clung to the phone's waterproof case, but otherwise, it was fine. Lucy edged her way out of the crowded room to answer it.

"We're both good," she told Nick. She glanced back into the room at Megan's beaming face, curls bouncing and hands gesturing as she told the story of her adventures that evening to Mateo and his family. Probably not for the first time. "But you should see your daughter flirting. It's shameless. We are so in trouble. I think we should rethink that whole convent thing. At least until she's thirty. Seriously."

Nick's laughter was a sound so pure and beautiful she fell in love with him every time she heard it. She turned to the tile wall, hiding her smile from everyone passing through the busy hospital corridor, cherishing this private moment in the midst of the chaos this day had delivered. No need to travel to the beach for sunshine; Nick was all the light she needed in this world.

"Well, she is her mother's daughter," he finally said. "And I wouldn't change that for anything."

ABOUT CJ:

New York Times and *USA Today* bestselling author of over forty novels, former pediatric ER doctor CJ Lyons has lived the life she writes about in her cutting edge Thrillers with Heart.

CJ has been called a "master within the genre" (Pittsburgh Magazine) and her work has been praised as "breathtakingly fast-paced" and "riveting" (Publishers Weekly) with "characters with beating hearts and three dimensions" (Newsday).

Her novels have twice won the International Thriller Writers' prestigious Thriller Award, the RT Reviewers' Choice Award, the Readers' Choice Award, the RT Seal of Excellence, and the Daphne du Maurier Award for Excellence in Mystery and Suspense.

Learn more about CJ's Thrillers with Heart at www.CJLyons.net

Printed by Amazon Italia Logistica S.r.l.
Torrazza Piemonte (TO), Italy

16990810R00098